STIRABOUT STORIES

Stirabout

Stories

brewed in her own cauldron by

BARBARA SLEIGH

ILLUSTRATED BY VICTOR AMBRUS

THE BOBBS-MERRILL COMPANY, INC.
Indianapolis   New York

For Hilary

THE BOBBS-MERRILL COMPANY, INC.
PUBLISHERS   INDIANAPOLIS   NEW YORK

Text copyright © 1971 by Barbara Sleigh
Illustrations copyright © 1971 by William Collins Sons & Co Ltd
First published in Great Britain by William Collins Sons & Co Ltd
in 1971 under the title of WEST OF WIDDERSHINS
Printed in the United States of America
Library of Congress catalog card number: 72–75888
0 9 8 7 6 5 4 3 2 1

Contents

Introduction

In my search for stories for *North of Nowhere*, I became increasingly aware of the earthy beginnings of all those tales which have been handed down so lovingly from generation to generation, in every country in the world. In most of them it is the things in common use in daily life that are invested with magic: the mirror on the wall; the cat on the hearth-rug; the spinning wheel in the corner; the fish drawn at random from the sea; the cooking pot and even the gin bottle. Wonderful things happen to both princes and peasants, to young and old, rich and poor.

Magic, it seems, no less than beauty, is in the eye of the beholder. But why should we feel that it must always be in period dress? Surely, if we look for it, it can be found in the classroom, in public parks, in anyone's back garden, even in supermarkets, just as much as in palaces and wood-cutters' huts?

In this collection of short stories I have tried to make a mixture in my cauldron of new as well as old, with a pinch of wonder and a handful of mystery, liberally laced with magic, and stirred, of course, anti-clockwise.

BARBARA SLEIGH

The Girl Who Got a Fairy in Her Eye

BRIDGET was running down the garden path when she got a fairy in her eye. When she blinked it out again, she wiped it carefully from her cheek on to the tip of her finger, where it clung, looking rather miserable, and draggled with wetness. It was no bigger than a bluebottle, and the palest green all over, from the soles of its feet to the top of its shining cap of hair. It was making what at first Bridget thought was a tiny buzzing noise, but when she held it close to her ear she realised it was talking, in a voice the size you would expect from a mosquito.

"Oh Bridgie! Bridgie!" it sighed. "Why did you have to get your great eye in the way?"

Although her eye was still sore, Bridget was so surprised that she did not say: "Why did you have to get in the way of my eye?" She only said: "I'm very sorry! I didn't see you coming."

"The very least you can do is to put me somewhere warm to dry, before I catch my death of cold."

As it spoke the Fairy sneezed, a sound no louder than the popping of a fuchsia bud. So very carefully Bridget put it on a daisy head in the sunshine, until it didn't look draggled any more, and from a dull grey its wings became faintly blue: the colour of her party hair ribbon.

"Deep shining kingfisher blue they should be," complained the Fairy. "It's the shock has turned them pale, and no wonder. One of them is broken, Bridgie, and it's all your fault! What are you going to do about it, my dear?"

Bridget could see that one wing was crumpled and hanging

down, but she did not feel that she was entirely to blame, so she said:

"If you are a fairy, could you not make a magic to cure it in a twinkling?"

"Out of the question!" said the Fairy sharply. "Have you ever heard of anyone making magic for themselves? It doesn't work. All we can do is grant a little matter of wishes to a few people . . ."

"Wishes?" said Bridget eagerly. "I've just broken my skipping rope, and I should so like a new one. I suppose you couldn't . . . ?"

"Grant you a wish?" said the Fairy, shaking its head. "Not yet awhile. Not in my present state of health. I should only get it muddled. When I've quite recovered, and my wings are once more a beautiful kingfisher blue, perhaps I might then. Who knows?"

"What can I do to make you well again?" asked Bridget.

"Well, first of all I should like something to drink," said the Fairy. "Faint with thirst I am!"

"I could get you a thimbleful of orange juice," said Bridget hopefully.

"No use at all," said the Fairy. "Too sweet."

"Then some water?" said Bridget.

"Not sweet enough," said the Fairy. "The only thing that would do me any good at all is a sip of greenfly milk. You know how to milk a greenfly, of course?"

"I'm afraid I don't," said Bridget.

"Well, go away and try!" said the Fairy impatiently.

Bridget found several greenflies crawling along a rose stem, looking, as greenflies usually do, so wan and weak that they might just have got out of bed from influenza. How to milk one she had not the slightest idea. So she sat on the grass and thought. While she was thinking she saw an ant. It was struggling to carry a grain of sand to the top of a little mound of soil that must have seemed as big as a mountain to him. But the grain of sand was so large and heavy for the little creature that he kept dropping it, so that it rolled to the bottom of the hill, and he had to start all over again. When Bridget had watched him fall back three times, with his load on top of him, she said:

"I'll carry your grain of sand to the top of the hill for you."

So she shovelled up the grain of sand with a blade of grass and put it on the top of the ant hill.

"Blessings on you, Human!" said the Ant. "What can I do to repay you?"

"I suppose you couldn't show me how to milk a greenfly?" asked Bridget doubtfully.

The Ant looked at the greenfly on the rose bush, and then at Bridget's hands, which must have looked as big as a giant's to so small an insect, and said:

"I'll do it myself and welcome, before you can say 'antennae'."

And in no time at all he ran up the rose tree, and milked the greenfly into an empty ant's egg. So Bridget thanked the Ant and took the greenfly milk to the Fairy. As it tilted up the egg shell with both hands, and drank the milk in half a dozen gulps, its wings turned a brighter, bluer blue: the colour of Bridget's brand new dressing gown.

"Do you feel well enough to grant me a wish now?" she asked.

"Oh, not yet awhile!" said the Fairy. "What about my poor

broken wing? The next thing is to find a splint to mend it with. What do you suggest?"

"A matchstick?" said Bridget uncertainly.

"Absurd!" said the Fairy. "Far too thick."

"A pin?" suggested Bridget.

"Ridiculous!" said the Fairy. "Far too sharp. Run away and look for something!"

"But where shall I look?" asked Bridget.

"Try a magpie's nest," said the Fairy. "You'll find plenty to choose from there."

Bridget went to the woody place over the garden wall, and gazed up through the tangle of branches of a hawthorn tree at a dark shape at the top that she thought might be a magpie's nest. Certainly there were two magpies circling round it, and the beat of their wings looked very strong, and their beaks very sharp and black. But because she began to get a crick in her neck from staring upwards, she put her head down and stared at the toes of her shoes instead. And by the toe of her right shoe she saw a stag beetle, lying on its back and waving its legs in the air in a desperate effort to turn on to its feet again. So very carefully Bridget turned him over with a stick, and the Stag Beetle said breathlessly:

"What a dreadful thing to happen! Helpless on my back and just below a magpie's nest! There's nothing a 'pie likes so much as a fine juicy stag beetle. How in the world can I ever thank you?"

"Could you help me find something in the magpies' nest?" said Bridget. "The trouble is I don't know what I am looking for until I see it. I could climb up to the nest, but that would take two hands, and the magpies might attack me before I have time to say that I don't want to hurt their eggs! And their wings look so very strong, and their beaks so very sharp and pointed!"

"Leave it to me!" said the Stag Beetle. "Do you climb up the tree and I will sit on your shoulder, and when you are nearly there I will lead them away. Oh, they'll follow all right. I told you, they find nothing so tasty as a stag beetle! But they won't catch me, not now I'm the right way up!"

Bridget climbed the hawthorn tree, up and up, and just before she reached the nest, rather scratched and with her dress torn, the magpies gave a harsh "Squark!" and dived down after the Stag Beetle, who dropped out of sight among the green leaves below her.

The nest had a dome of twigs woven over it, with a hole at the side through which the birds went in and out. Bridget peered cautiously through the hole, and there inside she found such odds and ends as you would hardly believe! There were sticks and straws and dead leaves, and brightly coloured bits of wool and cotton, and shreds of material, and silver toffee papers, and shining milk bottle tops: and nestling very comfortably in the middle were five greeny-bluey speckled eggs. But it was not the eggs in which Bridget was interested. Carefully woven among the sticks and straws was a fish's backbone, which might once have belonged to a kipper, with rows of slender little bones growing on either side.

"The very thing!" said Bridget, and she broke off a little fishbone and put it in her pocket, and climbed down the tree again and gave it to the Fairy.

"Not bad, Bridgie, my dear!" it said, preening its good wing, which was now as bright as the bluebag Bridget's mother used for washing. "Not bad at all!"

"Are you well enough now to grant me a wish?" asked Bridget once more. But the Fairy shook its shining green head and said:

"Oh, not yet awhile! My poor wing isn't mended. I'm still not well enough to make a wishing magic. Now find me something to tie the splint to my poor wing, and then ... who knows?"

"What shall I bring? A piece of wool?" asked Bridget.

"Not a bit of good!" said the Fairy. "Not firm enough."

"A piece of cotton?" suggested Bridget.

"Quite nonsensical!" said the Fairy. "Too coarse! There is

only one thing that is fine enough and strong enough, and that's a thread of gossamer!"

"But only spiders spin gossamer!" said Bridget, who was getting tired of being ordered about by something no bigger than her thumb nail.

"So they do!" said the Fairy. "Go to the first web you can find and ask the spider in residence to come back with you and bind the splint to my poor broken wing. Your great fingers would be far too clumsy. But before you go, Bridgie, please put me somewhere safe. Here was I lying helpless on a daisy head with only one wing in working order, when I was mistaken for a beetle by a blackbird! Quite sharp with him I had to be before he'd go away."

So Bridget put the Fairy in an empty match box on a bed of pink cotton wool, with the lid open so that it could breathe. Then she put the match box on the kitchen mantelpiece behind the clock, where no blackbird would ever discover it, and then she went to find a spider. She found one at last busy making a web, but when she explained what she wanted, the Spider, who had not paused in his spinning, simply said:

"Go away! Can't you see I'm busy? I'm behind time as it is." And then he scuttled away under a leaf on some private errand of his own.

Bridget stood wondering at the neatness of the web and the fineness of the gossamer, and just as she decided she must go away and find another, more obliging spider, a very small fly flew straight into the half-made web.

"Keep still," said Bridget to the Fly, who was floundering about in his efforts to free himself, and very carefully she unwound him from the web without breaking a single thread.

The Fly sat in the palm of her hand, panting slightly and fanning its wings.

"Oh, dear! Oh, dear!" it said. "What a narrow escape! It all comes of not looking where you are going. However can I thank you?"

"I suppose you couldn't tell me how to persuade the Spider to come with me and help to mend a fairy's broken wing?" asked Bridget.

"Nothing easier!" said the Fly. "You know that spiders always make their webs by running clockwise? Well, when he comes back, and begins to scuttle round and round, do you wave your finger at him, quite close, in the opposite direction until he stops, and you'll have him so mixed up he'll do anything you ask! All the same, I don't think I'll stay to watch. The very sight of a spider gives me the shudders!" And the Fly flew away with a "bizz".

Presently the Spider came back, and began running clockwise, round and round the web, weaving as he went, as though his life depended on it. When he had nearly finished the web, and was running in smaller and smaller circles, Bridget began twirling her finger round and round in the opposite direction, so close to him that she nearly touched, but not quite. After half a dozen twirls the Spider took two steps forward and one step back: and then he sat down, waving his forelegs in a distracted way.

"Stop it!" he said. "Stop it at once! You've got me so moithered I don't know which way I'm going!" And then he recognised Bridget. "So it's you again! I might have known it. All right, I'll come and mend your tiresome Fairy's wing if you promise to leave me alone then to get on with my web!"

So Bridget promised, and she put the Spider on a leaf, because she did not like the idea of holding him in her hand, and she fetched the match box from the kitchen mantelpiece, and woke the Fairy who was fast asleep.

"What a long time you've been!" it said, with a yawn. "I got quite tired of waiting. Come along, my good Spider. Be quick and mend my wing!"

"And never so much as a please or thank you!" said Bridget to herself as she watched the Spider bind the splint with gossamer. When he had done, he went off grumbling. But the Fairy said:

"Not bad, Bridgie, my dear! Not bad! I could even fly with it a little way!" And it stood up and stretched both wings which shimmered kingfisher blue in the sunshine.

"Then now you surely are well enough to grant me a wish?" said Bridget.

But the Fairy folded its wings at once and sat down as though it had suddenly come over faint.

"Not yet awhile, Bridgie," it said, putting its green head slyly on one side. "Now if you were to find me something to eat? A mere crumb of fresh honeycomb would do. Then perhaps I might . . ."

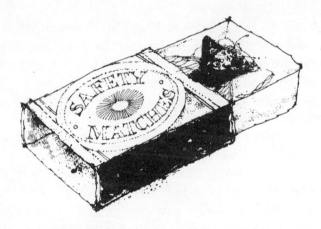

But here Bridget did something of which afterwards she was rather ashamed. She picked up the Fairy and put it in the match box, and closed the lid and said:

"There! Now I shall keep you shut up until you grant my wish! I've done everything you've asked me, and I don't believe you are a bit ill any more. You just want to keep me running errands for you!"

The Fairy buzzed angrily inside the match box, like a wasp in a jam jar. But Bridget took not a bit of notice. She put the box back on the kitchen mantelpiece, but because she was so busy being cross she forgot to put it behind the clock.

"I shall walk three times round the garden," she said. "And

then, if you will grant my wish, I will open the match box, and you may fly away."

When Bridget had walked round the garden once, very slowly, she stopped and said to herself:

"I forgot to make any holes in the match box lid. I do hope the Fairy can breathe!"

But her pride would not allow her to go indoors and look before she had been round the garden the three times she had promised. So she walked round the second time very fast. The third time she ran, and then she dashed into the kitchen. The match box was open, and there was nothing but pink cotton wool! The Fairy was gone. Her father had looked inside for a match to light his pipe, and something blue and buzzing had darted out, he said, and made a bee-line for the window before he could catch it, but not before it had given his finger a nasty nip.

Bridget was half glad and half sorry that the Fairy was gone. But the odd thing is that to make amends for letting the Fairy escape, her father made her a present of a new skipping rope, which you remember was just what she was going to wish for. To this day she cannot make up her mind if after all this was because the Fairy had relented and made a wishing magic.

The Four Golden Guinea-pigs

THIS is the tale of four golden guinea-pigs with ruby eyes, who
lived in a milk-white guinea-pig sty, and their names were:

Pemberton

Emberton

Berton

and Ton.

They spent their days whiffling their noses, and counting the
little white clouds that drifted across the square of blue sky they
could see above them. When they grew tired of this, in their
shrill guinea-pig voices, they sang a song they had made up,
which went like this:

> "*Golden guinea-pigs four are we,*
> *Wise and witty as all agree.*
> *The cleverest animals under the sun,*
> *Pemberton, Emberton, Berton and Ton.*

Twice a day a great Hand came down from the sky and fed
them with food and water.

One morning, when it had rained for nearly two whole weeks, and the square of sky had been like a dull grey blanket stretched overhead, there had been no little white clouds to count. They could not sing their song because Pemberton had got his feet wet, and he was so hoarse that all he could do was to beat time. Without him they made no more noise than the squeaking of a rusty hinge, for he had a fine singing voice – for a guinea-pig.

"No clouds to count! No song to sing!" said Berton.

"Surely there is something else to do besides whiffle our noses all day?" said Emberton.

And Ton, who although he was the youngest and smallest, was by far the most daring, said:

"For a long time I have wanted to look and see what is on the other side of our milk-white wall!"

"Ooooh!" said his brothers, throwing up their little pink paws in wonderment. "Do you think we dare?"

Ton did not answer, but he pushed the upturned food bowl against the milk-white wall, and he rolled the water jar up on top of that, and because it was still not high enough, for he was a very small guinea-pig, with some difficulty he balanced an old cabbage stalk on top of the water jar, and when he stood on *that*, by hanging on to the top of the wall with both paws he could just see over to the other side, and his ruby eyes grew even rounder with surprise at what he saw.

"You'll never believe me!" said Ton. "But the sky isn't square after all!"

"Not square?" echoed his brothers. "Then what shape is it?"

"It's not a shape exactly," said Ton. "It's like a great, huge upside-down drinking bowl."

Pemberton, Emberton and Berton found this so hard to believe that they scrambled up beside Ton to see for themselves.

"Whooo!" said Pemberton in an awed voice. "How very big is this over-the-wall place!"

"Whooo! I think I can see another animal over there!" said

Emberton. "But it's not a bit like us. It's got a great long thing hanging down behind!"

"Perhaps he doesn't know it's there," said Berton.

"In which case it would be a kindness to tell him," said Ton.

So he called out in a voice that was surprisingly loud – for such a small guinea-pig: "Hi there! My good animal!"

And the creature looked up and said angrily:

"Don't you 'my good animal' me! I'm a self-respecting mouse come foraging for my family! Who are you to give yourself airs, and what do you want?"

"Just to tell you that you have a great long thing stuck on to you behind," said Ton.

The Mouse turned his head and looked, and saw nothing but his tail.

"If you think that's funny, I'm not a mouse to stand cheek from anyone!" And he bared his white teeth at them. But Pemberton, Emberton and Berton twittered in their high guinea-pig voices that it wasn't cheek, and indeed they had only meant to be helpful.

"I'm almost inclined to believe you," said the Mouse at last, looking up at the four pairs of ruby eyes peering down at him over the milk-white wall. "Who are you who don't know a tail when you see one?"

And the four brothers lifted up their heads and sang:

"*Golden guinea-pigs four are we,*
Wise and witty as all agree.
The cleverest animals under the sun,
Pemberton, Emberton, Berton and Ton!"

"Guinea-pigs? I never heard tell of such creatures. Haven't you got tails hanging down like all other animals?"

The four guinea-pigs turned round to look, and Pemberton said:

"Where Mouse has a tail, we have . . . a nothingness!"

But when they turned back again to tell the Mouse of this surprising discovery, it had gone.

"Did he say that *all* other animals have tails?" said Pemberton uneasily.

"And is it wrong of us not to have them?" said Emberton.

But Ton replied:

"It is far more likely that we are right and all of the others are wrong! Are we not the cleverest animals under the sun? And anyway, we have only the Mouse's word for it. I'm going to see for myself!" And as he spoke he scrambled over the milk-white wall. Pemberton, Emberton and Berton tried to grab him back, but in so doing they all three fell over themselves.

"Whooo!" they said, looking anxiously about them. "This over-the-wall place is even bigger than we thought! Who knows what strange things we shall find here? Perhaps animals with two tails or more!"

"Courage, brothers!" said Ton. "Never forget who we are!" and he hummed the tune of their song to remind them, "And that it is far superior to have a nothingness than a tail. If there is any talking to be done, leave it all to me!"

They set out, four abreast, and presently they met a Rabbit.

"A very fine morning to you!" said the Rabbit. "But who are you? I never saw creatures like you before."

The four brothers sat up on their haunches and sang:

> *Golden guinea-pigs four are we,*
> *Wise and witty as all agree.*
> *The cleverest animals under the sun,*
> *Pemberton, Emberton, Berton and Ton!"*

"That may be," said the Rabbit. "But excuse me. Have you had an accident or something? A trap or a train, perhaps? To cut off all your tails, I mean?"

Ton nudged his brothers to stop them saying humbly that they just did not happen to have any tails, and said:

"Accident? No such thing! What should we want with such a common object as a tail? A thing that everyone else has! We have a nothingness instead, and that is very much grander!"

"Dear me," said the Rabbit. "I didn't know it was common

to have a tail." And she looked back anxiously at her little white scut, and hopped away and sat herself down in the muddiest puddle she could find.

"What are you doing that for?" asked her friends.

"I'm covering my scut with mud so that I hope it won't show any more. I don't want to look as though I have anything so common as a tail!"

"Tails common?" said the Rabbit's friends. "We didn't know. Make room for us as well in your puddle."

Meanwhile the brothers went on their way, four abreast, feeling rather pleased with themselves, and the next animal they met was a Squirrel, who threw a nut at them from the branch of a tree on which he was sitting, and called out:

"Hi! What kind of animal are you? I've never seen the likes of you before!"

And the brothers sat up on their haunches and sang rather louder than before:

"Golden guinea-pigs four are we,
Wise and witty as all agree.
The cleverest animals under the sun,
Pemberton, Emberton, Berton and Ton!"

The Squirrel jumped down from the tree to examine them more closely, and he began to shake with laughter.

"Excuse me laughing!" he said. "But you look so funny without any tails!"

"Funny?" said Ton scornfully. "My good animal, it is you who look funny with that great clumsy thing sticking up behind. Didn't you know that tails went out of fashion weeks ago? It is far grander to wear a nothingness as we do!"

"Tails not fashionable?" said the Squirrel. "I'm much obliged to you for telling me. I had no idea." And he looked round anxiously at his fine bushy tail and rolled it up into a tight little ball.

"What are you doing that for?" asked his squirrel friends.

"Trying to look as though I have a nothingness, of course, now that tails are out of fashion."

"Tails out of fashion?" said his friends, and they rolled their fine bushy tails up too.

The four guinea-pigs swaggered on their way, and the next animal they met was a Dog.

The Dog wagged his short tail, and cocked his head at them in a friendly, inquisitive way. But the four brothers sat up on their haunches, and without being invited, sang very loudly indeed:

> *"Golden guinea-pigs four are we,*
> *Wise and witty as all agree.*
> *The cleverest animals under the sun,*
> *Pemberton, Emberton, Berton and Ton!"*

And Ton went on grandly: "And we've come to tell you that tails are simply not worn this year. In fact, it is not considered polite even to use the word!"

"You don't say!" said the Dog in astonishment. "Tails – I mean those things we don't mention – not worn any more?"

"Certainly not!" said Ton haughtily. "Only an elegant nothing-ness!"

"I see that's what you wear yourselves," said the Dog humbly. "It's very good of you grand gentlemen to come and tell me." And he hurriedly lowered his tail and tucked it between his back legs. "How surprised the others will be when I tell them!"

"No doubt they will," said Ton graciously. And the brothers strutted on their way, four abreast, with their chests so puffed out with pride that they could hardly see where they were going.

By this time it was evening, and they were a long way from home.

"I'm growing very hungry," said Pemberton.

"The Hand is late with our food and water," said Emberton.

"We are travelling so fast that perhaps it can't keep up with us," said Berton.

"In that case perhaps we had better wait under this hedge for it to catch up," said Ton.

And so the four guinea-pigs waited under the hedge . . . but no Hand came. The sun set and night came on and they huddled together to keep themselves warm, and although they were hungrier still by morning, their spirits rose with the sun.

"Courage, brothers!" said Ton. "I think I see another animal over there who must be told how misguided he is to wear a tail."

"It is a very big tail!" said Pemberton.

"Joined on to a very big animal!" said Emberton.

"Do you think we dare?" said Berton.

"Pooh!" said Ton. "Have we not shown Rabbit, Squirrel and Dog how wrong they have all been? Are we to be put off just because a misguided animal is large? Be brave, and follow me!"

So Pemberton, Emberton and Berton followed Ton as he strutted up to the Cow, for that was what the animal was, and without waiting for the Cow to speak they sat up on their haunches and sang in the very loudest voices they could manage:

"Golden guinea-pigs four are we,
Wise and witty as all agree.
The cleverest animals under the sun,
Pemberton, Emberton, Berton and Ton!"

But the Cow took no notice at all. She just went on eating the juicy green grass. A little puzzled, the four brothers began to sing again. But no sooner had they begun than the Cow looked up and said with her mouth full of dandelion:

"All right, all right! You needn't bother. I heard you the first time. *And* yesterday evening over the hedge, telling Dog all that nonsense about tails being out of fashion! If I was you I should look behind you!"

Pemberton, Emberton, Berton and Ton did as they were told, and across the field came running towards them: four dogs, twenty squirrels and more rabbits than you could possibly count, and they arranged themselves in a not very friendly circle with the four golden guinea-pigs in the middle.

"And who said so?" went on the Cow.

"Said what?" asked Ton uncomfortably.

"As you was 'the cleverest animals under the sun'?"

Ton thought for a minute, and then he said in a small voice: "Well, I suppose we did!"

"Clever!" said the Cow, "when you don't even know what tails is for! If I was to pretend I had no tail, like some silly animals I could name, how do you think I could flick off them varmints of flies?"

"Oh!" said Ton. "We hadn't thought of that."

"And there's a lot of other things you haven't thought of," went on Dog. "How in the world can I show my master how pleased I am to see him without a tail to wag? Because I pretended I hadn't got one, he thought I was ill, and gave me some medicine. Horrible, it was!"

"And how can I keep my balance when I leap from branch to branch?" asked the Squirrel. "Bruised all over I am with trying to jump without one."

"And how are my children to follow me without a white scut to shine in the twilight?" said the Rabbit. "Three of them got lost last night, and it's no thanks to you silly creatures that they didn't get eaten by a Fox!"

"I'm very sorry!" said Ton humbly. "I didn't know that tails were useful, not having such things ourselves . . ."

"Then," said the Cow, "if you have no tails I suppose you don't lead your children through the dusk, or climb trees, or wag something to show you are pleased, or flick away them pesky flies. If it isn't asking too much, what in the world do you do all day?"

"Whooo!" said Pemberton. "We whiffle our noses!"

"And count the little white clouds as they drift over the sky!" said Emberton eagerly.

"And we sing our song, of course!" said Berton.

And the four brothers were just sitting up on their haunches to sing it over again, when the Cow blew down her nose so scornfully and so hard that they were knocked head over heels backwards. When they picked themselves up again the crowd of animals were all going away about their separate businesses, in a forest of waving tails. Only the Dog remained. He looked at them with his head inquisitively on one side, wagging his tail in a friendly way, and said: "What now, little creatures?"

"Alas, we have been very foolish, conceited animals," said Pemberton, Emberton and Berton. "And although it is a little comfort to know that we do not need to have tails, we can't help feeling ashamed that we are the only ones to have a nothingness."

But Ton said:

"The only thing I have room to feel at this present moment is a very great hungriness. Sir Dog, can you, of your kindness, tell us when and where the great Hand will come down from the sky and bring us food and water? We haven't seen it since we left our milk-white guinea-pig sty a long while ago, and we are very, very empty!"

"Then I should go back to your milk-white guinea-pig sty," said the Dog. "My Hand only comes to feed me by my own back door. Creatures of habit, humans."

"Humans?" said the four golden guinea-pigs.

"You'll find one joined on to your great Hand if you look," said the Dog.

"Whooo!" said the brothers, holding up their little pink front paws in surprise. And they scuttled away to their guinea-pig sty to see for themselves. They scrambled over the milk-white wall, and in a very short time the great Hand came down from the sky and stroked them, and they looked for the first time and, lo and behold, a Boy was joined on to it!

"I'm so glad you've come back!" said the Boy. "I was afraid

you had gone away for ever. I'll go and fetch you some food and water this very minute!"

The four golden guinea-pigs watched him go with their round ruby eyes, and Ton said:

"Did you notice something, brothers?"

And Pemberton, Emberton and Berton said:

"The Boy has no tail either! He has nothing but a nothingness just like us!"

"So we aren't the only ones, after all!" said Ton. "And that makes all the difference!"

Never again did the four brothers scramble over their milk-white wall. They spent the days contentedly whiffling their noses and counting the little white clouds that drifted over the blue sky above them, and sometimes they sang their song. The tune was the same, but the words were a little different.

"*Golden guinea-pigs four are we,*" they sang in their shrill guinea-pig voices,

> "*Not very clever as all will agree.*
> *In modest humility second to none,*
> *Pemberton, Emberton, Berton and Ton!*"

But sometimes, just sometimes, Ton would go into a corner by himself and sing the old words in a tiny voice that no one else could hear:

> "*Golden guinea-pigs four are we,*
> *Wise and witty as all agree.*
> *The cleverest animals under the sun,*
> *Pemberton, Emberton, Berton and Ton!*"

Miss Peabody

ONCE upon a time there was a teacher called Miss Peabody, and a class called Lower 3a.

After the strange things that happened one summer term, Lower 3a were never quite sure if Miss Peabody was a witch, but they decided they had better be a little bit careful, just in case. You never know with witches. Lower 3a was just the kind of class which can make teachers very cross indeed in the shortest possible time.

Miss Peabody could have told them exactly how the strange things came about. But of course she never did. It all began with her headaches. Usually her lessons were interesting enough to keep any class from being naughty: especially history. But if she had one of her headaches they became very dull indeed, and then of course, Lower 3a enlivened them with all the old dodges. They talked and giggled: they made long visits to the cloakroom to fetch handkerchiefs which were not there: they put up-ended drawing pins on one another's chairs, and ate a special kind of wine gum that they thought, mistakenly, could be sucked without anyone knowing.

This particular Summer Term the Mayor had offered a prize to the group in any school which made the best model illustrating something in history. Miss Peabody got quite excited. So did Lower 3a. They began to make a model of old London Bridge, with paper mashed up in paste, and poster paint, and shiny crinkled paper for the River Thames.

Lower 3a were working very hard and Miss Peabody was

pleased with them, when one of her headaches started, and then another, and another. And from a class of keen young model-makers, Lower 3a became a giggling, inattentive rabble. Paint water was upset, up-ended drawing pins appeared all over the place, and the sweet shop completely ran out of wine gums because they bought so many. Of course the model of old London Bridge began to suffer.

"I shall *have* to go to the doctor about these headaches," said Miss Peabody to herself. "But not to Doctor Simson this time. Supposing Bobby Simson saw me sitting in the surgery? The whole of Lower 3a would know about it in the morning, and goodness knows how it might make them giggle! I shall take a bus ticket to the end of the bus route and go to the first doctor I can find."

When she left the bus Miss Peabody had to walk quite a long way, so that it was dusk before she found a doctor. There was not enough light to read his name on the brass plate outside, but there was a red light over the door.

"How old-fashioned!" said Miss Peabody to herself. For that is how doctors showed their trade a long time ago.

The doctor sat at his desk. There was only the light of a reading lamp in the surgery, but she could see that three of the walls were covered with ancient books, with powdery leather bindings. There were, as well, some scales and a sight-testing card, and hanging over the desk, to her surprise, was a stuffed alligator.

"How very odd!" said Miss Peabody to herself. "Almost as if . . ."

"As if what?" repeated the doctor looking up for the first time, and although he was the oldest old man Miss Peabody had ever seen, his eyes were surprisingly young and bright. "If there is a stuffed toad in the science room of Birch Road Junior School, why should I not have a stuffed alligator in my surgery? Now about these headaches of yours . . ." Miss Peabody gave a little gasp, for she had said never a word out loud about either head-aches or alligators or Birch Road Junior School, but the doctor went on: "It seems that children are much the same as they have always been."

"But Lower 3a . . ." began Miss Peabody.

"*I* know," broke in the doctor. "Drawing pins and wine gums and the rest. I think a little Wishing Tonic may be what you need, and no doubt it will do Lower 3a a little good as well."

As he spoke he wrote on his prescription pad, in the usual doctor's unreadable writing, and handed the little slip of paper to Miss Peabody. "Good day to you," he said. "Next patient, please!"

The chemist looked a little puzzled when she handed him the prescription.

"I don't think I've ever been asked for this before," he said. But the medicine looked quite ordinary when he had made it up. It was in two tiny bottles. The label on one said: "An egg shell full to be taken after breakfast." The liquid was red. The other was green as grass. The label on this just said "The Antidote".

"To undo the first medicine, I suppose. How very odd!"

Miss Peabody could hardly wait for next day. She woke with the worst possible headache. The medicine hissed slightly when she poured it into the newly washed shell of her breakfast egg, and a little nervously she shut her eyes and swallowed it down. It was sweet and syrupy, and it sent a tingling glow from her toes to her finger tips, but when she opened her eyes her head hurt as much as ever.

"How I wish it would cure the pain!" said Miss Peabody.

And at once it did. Her headache had quite gone – "As if by magic!" she said. And then she caught sight of the clock. "Goodness, how late it is! And it's pouring with rain. I wish I was at school!"

And at once she was: sitting in her desk in Lower 3a classroom, breathing a little quickly, and with her hair rather blown about. Willy Brown and Nora Smith, who had come to school early to arrange some up-ended drawing pins, were staring at her with their mouths open. Miss Peabody saw what they were up to, but she said to herself:

"It's happened twice! I said 'I wish . . .' and my headache went, and I said it again and it whisked me here! It *must* be magic!" Aloud she said:

"How splendid of you to come early to get on with your work, Nora and Willy. When you've picked up all those drawing pins someone seems to have spilled, you may fill the paint pots with water for me."

"Yes, Miss Peabody," said Nora and Willy meekly.

It was only when she reached the door that she realised that she was still wearing her bedroom slippers. They were scarlet with yellow pom-poms. Nora was staring at them with round eyes, but she did not giggle. Miss Peabody wished the magic had given her time to change. It was all rather difficult to explain when she had to borrow a pair of gym shoes from the gym teacher.

Lessons began as usual. Although Lower 3a felt that there was something different about Miss Peabody, being naughty had become a habit. When they were doing sums there were spurts of giggling, and presently there was the unmistakable smell of someone sucking wine gums.

"Who is eating sweets?" asked Miss Peabody.

Barry Jones and Sara Robinson put up their hands. Several others looked a little uncomfortable.

"Put them in the wastepaper basket at once," said Miss Peabody. "You know, if all the sweets this class has eaten during lessons this term were put end to end, you would be surprised how far they would stretch. I wish you could see them!"

And at once they could. There was a line of sweets stretching from Miss Peabody's desk, down the classroom and round the corner, right to the door. There were wine gums and jelly babies and chocolate bars, and liquorice boot laces and hundreds-and-thousands and peppermint lumps and assorted toffees galore.

"Leave them where they are," said Miss Peabody. "And perhaps the sight of them will make you feel a little ashamed!"

There was no more giggling. Lower 3a went on with their work without a sound.

Ten minutes later Mr Hammock the headmaster opened the door.

"Miss Peabody," he said coldly. "There is a trail of sweets leading from your classroom right down the passage and round the corner to the door of my study. I suppose Lower 3a is responsible?"

Lower 3a all held their breaths as they waited for Miss Peabody's answer.

"Oh, no," she said after a moment's pause. "It was entirely my doing. A little experiment in – er, arithmetic."

Lower 3a breathed again. Good old Poddy, they thought! They had been rather beastly to her lately, but she hadn't given them away!

"I think such practical experiments should be carried out inside the classroom in future," said Mr Hammock, and stalked away on his long legs.

"Barry and Sara, please take the wastepaper basket and collect all the sweets in the passage," said Miss Peabody. "And don't eat a single one! I shall know if you do." (Goodness knows what they might turn into if they did eat them!) "How thoughtless this magic business is!" she went on to herself. "Bringing me to school in my bedroom slippers, and no hat or coat on a wet day like this, and taking the sweets to Mr Hammock's door, of all people! I shall have to be very careful of saying 'I wish,' without thinking."

But it was more easily said than done.

Miss Peabody was careful for several days, and then, in the middle of a lesson on geography, a button came off Susan Pollock's cuff. John Tomkins, who sat next to her, already had a shirt button in his pencil box, so that a game of Tiddleywinks seemed the natural thing to do with them. One or two others thought it rather a good idea, and if they had not a button handy, they pulled one off where it would not show. They were so busy about it that John and Sara did not see Miss Peabody standing behind them.

"Give me those buttons, please," she said. Then hearing the snick of another Tiddleywinks player she added: "I wish to have all the buttons in the room on my desk, please!"

She meant of course all the *loose* buttons in the room, but that was not what she had said. There was a pause, and then the air was filled with a number of little poppings, like the bursting of gorse buds on a hot June day, followed by the patter of small hard things falling like rain on the lid of Miss Peabody's desk.

"That wishing magic again!" she said to herself, and went on wildly: "Counting fifteen buttons to each child, that makes 775!"

And then the bell went for the next lesson.

"You must go to the gym now," she said aloud. "And when you come back you can sew them all on again."

"But we can't go to gym like this!" said George almost tearfully, holding up his trousers with both hands.

Miss Peabody looked at Lower 3a, all holding their clothes together, without a single button between them, and said: "Perhaps you're right. Instead of gym we shall just have to have a sewing lesson. Boys as well as girls."

But there was worse to come. It was Miss Peabody's turn for dinner duty that day with the whole school, together with Miss Price. It was boiled cod, white and watery. George was sitting on her right, and Patty, who hated fish in any form, on her left. To distract Miss Peabody, while Patty got rid of her cod, George said:

"Miss Peabody, what did people eat in the days of old London Bridge?"

"An Elizabethan feast, you mean? Well, I expect it would taste a little odd to us," said Miss Peabody, turning to George, while Patty thankfully shovelled the cod into her handkerchief. "But I expect it would be delicious when you got used to it. I only wish you could taste one!"

The noise of 120 children talking, and the clatter of 120 knives and forks stopped as suddenly as though it had been turned off by a tap. The checked tablecloths were gone, and the thick white plates and the mangled pieces of cod. Instead, in the centre of the long polished table that had taken the place of the chipped deal one provided by the school, was a large model of the school crest, an owl in a mortarboard, all made of sugar. In front of each boy and girl was a shining pewter plate and a large tankard, and up and down the table were huge dishes of wonderful fruit: peaches and cherries, oranges and strawberries. There were sugar plums and suckets, and piles of sweetmeats, and marzipan that made the mouth water. The door opened and the kitchen staff filed in, looking a little puzzled, but bearing great dishes on high. Miss Peabody rose excitedly.

"Roast peacock!" she cried. "And venison pasty, and sucking pig and marrowbone pie! A real Elizabethan feast, dears, this is wonderful! The only way to teach history! Why did I not think of it before? Come along, children, eat it up!"

"But we've no knives or forks!" said Sally Wilkinson.

"Of course not, dear!" said Miss Peabody. "Use your fingers! That's what everyone did in the days of old London Bridge! Eat up your sucking pig, Henry! And Pamela, no jumbals or suckets till you have finished your nice stewed pike! I'm sure it's delicious, cooked in wine and cream. Those black things it is stuffed with, William? Why, prunes, of course!"

Gingerly Birch Road Junior School tasted the strange food before them, and as they found most of it good they took heart and tucked in manfully, while Miss Peabody urged them on. She had quite forgotten Miss Price, who suddenly took her firmly by the arm, at the same time holding up an enormous tankard.

"What is the liquid in this?" she asked. Miss Peabody peered and smelt and tasted, and then she said impatiently:

"Malmsey wine, of course . . . Well no, perhaps they had better not drink that. Billy dear, put that tankard down!"

"But Miss Peabody, it all looks so indigestible, don't you think?" said Miss Price. "To-morrow . . ."

"To-morrow," said Miss Peabody triumphantly, "I shall take the whole of Lower 3a to Elizabethan England! What an opportunity!"

Miss Peabody was so excited by the idea that she did not notice Miss Price hurry from the room. Fifteen minutes later the dishes were almost bare, and Birch Road Juniors, unbelievably sticky and very full indeed, were languidly eating the last of the sugar owl, when the door opened and Mr Hammock came in, followed by Miss Price, and Mrs Honey who cooked the school dinners. Mrs Honey was in tears.

"I never did, sir!" she was saying. "Cod I cooked for to-day! Boiled with parsley sauce. Not them horrible messes!"

She pointed to the remains of the peacock and the marrowbone pie.

Now Miss Peabody was very sorry to think that she had

caused Mrs Honey distress. Many times she had made Miss Peabody a nice strong cup of tea, when she had a headache. Had the magic done it again?

"Please don't cry, Mrs Honey," she said. "It was entirely my doing."

"Then," said Mr Hammock icily, "I am very sorry to hear it! As you know I am always in favour of practical teaching, but this is carrying things too far!"

"But, Mr Hammock, don't you see?" said Miss Peabody. "These children have had a history lesson they will never forget! How I wish I was a child again with them . . ."

She stopped, her hand over her mouth. But it was too late. Before the astonished eyes of Mr Hammock, Miss Price, Mrs Honey, and all the pupils of Birch Road Junior School, she began to shrink. She herself felt as if she was going down, rather too quickly, in a lift which stopped with a jolt, and left her staring at the bottom button of Mr Hammock's waistcoat, instead of his surprised blue eyes. Then she noticed a chilliness about her knees. With a gasp of dismay she watched her sensible tweed skirt shrink and fade into a very short gym tunic. Something was tickling her neck. She put her hand up and felt the ribbons on the end of two rather thin plaits.

Mr Hammock's face, now tilted down at her, looked dazed.

"I can't quite remember the class you are in, my dear," he said uncertainly. "But I will see you in my study. Immediately!" he added, pulling himself together.

Miss Peabody rushed from the dining-room, but not to Mr Hammock's study. She dashed down the passage and out of the front door. Along the drive she ran, her plump knees twinkling, along the High Street, down Percy Avenue, with one thing only in her mind, the second bottle of medicine! She was not trusting to any more wishes. Down her own road she pelted, through the front door and up the stairs to her room. She snatched up the bottle with its liquid, green as grass, and tossed it all off in one gulp. It burnt her throat and made her cough. She shut her eyes and counted twenty. The same curious "lift" feeling began again, but this time going up. Then she opened her eyes and looked in the mirror. Never had she gazed at her own ordinary but grown-up reflection with such pleasure! Then she took a deep breath – and wished she was back at school again. Nothing happened. Miss Peabody gave a sigh of relief.

A few of the Birch Road Junior School children were rather unwell in the night, but nobody ever referred to that afternoon again: not even Mr Hammock. Lower 3a did win the Mayor's Prize after all. Miss Peabody never had another headache and Lower 3a were seldom naughty, at least, not in Miss Peabody's lessons. As far as I know there has been no more magic at Birch Road Junior School: though there was a rumour that Winifred Potts had seen Miss Peabody whirl past the cloakroom window on a broomstick late one evening, when she had been kept in. But you know how stories get about in school.

Princess Peridot's Choice

THERE were once three princesses, and their names were Miranda, Fleurette and Peridot. Miranda, who was the eldest, was just fifteen.

One morning, they had all three kicked off their high-heeled shoes, and hitched up their velvet skirts the better to play hop-scotch on the marble terrace in front of the palace, when up came their old Nurse.

"For shame! For shame!" she said. "The three of you jumping about like frogs in a pond, instead of grown-up princess young ladies, with your hair all blowzy, and your skirts all towzled, and His Majesty the King wanting the Princess Miranda in the Golden Throne Room this very minute!"

"The Golden Throne Room!" said Miranda. "Then it must be for something very important. Do tell us what it is!"

The old Nurse nodded importantly, like someone who could tell a great deal if they chose, but all she said was:

"You'll know soon enough! But you'd better look as pretty as you're able, so come you here."

She took a comb from her pocket and tugged at Miranda's untidy hair, and tweaked her velvet skirt into place and sent her packing.

Miranda was away a long time. When she came back she was walking very slowly.

"What was it?" asked Fleurette.

"Tell us!" said Peridot.

"I am to be married quite soon," she said. "There were six

young princes in the Golden Throne Room and I had to say which one I wanted to be my husband. They were all rich and handsome, and there didn't seem a pin to choose between them."

"Then what did you do?" asked Peridot.

"I chose the one whose whiskers were longer and more curling than the others."

"But why are you so miserable?" asked Fleurette.

"Because after I had chosen I found that my prince was very, very dull. But I have given my royal word, and so I must marry him."

And marry him she did, with trumpets trumpeting, and flags flying, and everyone enjoying themselves like anything – except the Princess Miranda.

"You won't catch *me* marrying someone because of his long curling whiskers!" said Peridot. "Not I!"

A few months later Fleurette and Peridot were playing Cat's Cradle together with a silver thread – this is a game that two can play – when the old Nurse came bustling up again.

"Now *that's* a much more ladylike way of passing the time," she said. "This time it's Princess Fleurette His Majesty the King has summoned to the Golden Throne Room."

She tweaked the ruffles at Fleurette's throat, and bade her polish the toes of her scarlet slippers on the backs of her stockings and sent her packing.

After a while Fleurette returned, walking as slowly as her sister had done.

"Yes, I'm to be married too, quite soon," she said. "There were six young princes I had never seen before, and I had to choose between them. They were all equally rich and handsome."

"Then how did you decide? asked Peridot.

"I chose the one with the grandest moustache," said Fleurette. "I did not find out till later that he was very, very conceited; but I had given my word, and so I must marry him."

And marry him she did, and the fountains ran wine for the grown-ups, and lemonade for the children, and everyone laughed and feasted, and enjoyed themselves no end – except Fleurette.

"You won't catch *me* marrying someone because of his grand moustache!" said Peridot. "Not I!"

Time went by, and Princess Peridot was playing Patience – Patience is a card game that you can play by yourself. The old Nurse was sitting beside her with a great pile of mending, for even Princesses wear holes in their stockings. She knew that Peridot was lonely without her sisters.

"I'm sick of playing games by myself!" said Peridot presently.

The old Nurse nodded and bit off her thread. "Well, by all I hear, you won't have to play by yourself much longer. There's such a scrubbing and a polishing going on in the Golden Throne Room that it will be your turn for a husband any day now I shouldn't wonder!"

"But I don't want to marry a husband like either of my sisters," said Peridot.

"Well, what more do you want, pray?" said the old Nurse indignantly. "Such handsome upstanding young gentlemen, and rich into the bargain!"

Peridot dealt herself another card, and it was the Ace of Hearts.

"One of them is dull, and the other is conceited. I want a great deal more in my husband than that," said Peridot, fiddling with the Ace of Hearts in her agitation.

She pushed the game of Patience away and went out into the garden. Without thinking she had put the Ace of Hearts in her pocket.

When Princess Peridot was unhappy, she always took refuge in the garden. The thing she liked doing best in the world was to tie a great coarse apron over her grand clothes and grub about in her own small flower bed. Even the Head Gardener had to admit that her larkspurs were a deeper blue, and her roses more scented, than those in the rest of the palace gardens; but this time the flowers brought her no comfort. It was all very well to say she would never be so silly as her sisters, and choose a husband just because his whiskers curled, but how in the world was she to make a sensible choice if she knew nothing of the princes who asked for her hand?

Peridot wandered on, deep in thought, until she came to a part of the garden she had never been to before. Hidden away behind a hedge of privet there was a potting shed with a jumble of flower pots beside it, and a bonfire burning lazily in the summer sunshine. She up-ended the largest flower pot and sat down with her chin in her hand to think the better. The bonfire interrupted her thoughts by suddenly giving a great puff of smoke. When it cleared, what should she see but a little old man in a green baize apron poking the fire with a stick, so that the flames danced again. His face was as brown and wrinkled as an acorn cup, and his ears beneath his old felt hat were oddly pointed.

"Are you one of the gardeners?" she asked. "I don't think I've seen you before."

"Summat like that," said the little man. "There's more to growing green things than a pocket of earth and a pipkin of water."

Peridot agreed, and the old man and the young princess began to talk about gardening. They talked of planting and pruning, of mulches and marrows and marigolds, as gardeners will. Presently the old man said:

"You'm a proper one for growing green things. I've seen your tiddy little flower bed, and I know. Now, when I first clapped eyes on you sitting there, you was as pale as a stick of celery, and drooping like a bit of parched rhubarb. What's the matter, eh?"

Peridot told the old man about her two sisters, and how they had chosen their husbands, and how she had no idea of how to make a better choice herself. As she talked she could not help a couple of tears trickling down her cheeks, so she pulled her handkerchief out of her pocket, and as she did so the playing card fluttered down to the ground. The little man picked it up, and when he saw it was the Ace of Hearts, he chuckled.

"You're in luck, my dear! This here card is the very thing! There's not so many born gardeners in the world as we can afford

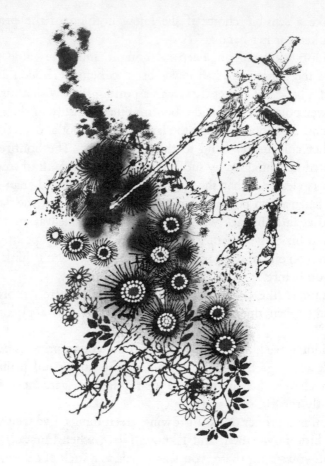

to lose one of 'em. Marry the wrong chap and maybe you'll not be allowed to touch fork nor trowel again. Now just you do as I bid and you won't go wrong!"

As he spoke, with one gnarled finger he pressed on the back of the playing card, and with a "pop" like a cork from a bottle, the little crimson heart in the centre shot into the air. He caught it deftly with one brown hand and slapped it down on the back of the other and held it out to Peridot.

"Here you are, my dear. Put it to soak overnight in the greenest puddle water you can find, and in the morning, just before sun-up, plant it in a golden flower pot with a silver trowel, in soil that is not too moist and not too dry, and when the blooms are fully out and the scent is ripe, make each young prince chap smell one of the flowers."

"But how will that help me?" asked Peridot.

"There's more to some flowers than a splodge of colour and a twirl of petals," said the old man, nodding gravely.

As he spoke there was a great puff of smoke from the bonfire which made Peridot's eyes smart, and when she had rubbed them clear again there was no sign of the little man; but there was the cardboard heart in the palm of her hand.

So she soaked it overnight in the greenest puddle water she could find. In the morning it was cardboard no longer, but plump and round as a crocus bulb. When the first cock crowed, just before the sun rose, she planted it in a golden flower pot with a silver trowel, in soil that was not too moist and not too dry.

"Huh!" said the old Nurse. "Making mud pies at your time of life, when this very evening, they say, you must go to the Golden Throne Room to choose your husband!"

"This evening!" said Peridot to herself. "Oh, dear, there is no plant in the world that will flower on the same day that it is planted!"

But as she looked there was a stirring in the golden flower pot, and a pale shoot nosed its way through the soil that was not too moist and not too dry. By the time she had finished her breakfast the shoot was strong and green and six inches high: by the time she had eaten her dinner it was eighteen inches high. She watched it all afternoon, and saw the leaf buds swell and burst and shake out their green leaves like tiny flags. When she had finished her tea the plant was tall and slender, and crowned with six curved stems, growing like the spokes of a wheel, and hanging from the tip of each stem was a crimson, heart-shaped flower bud the size of a hazel nut; but there was no scent.

"Come along, my dear," said the old Nurse. "You are summoned to the Golden Throne Room this very minute. Such rich handsome young princes as you'll have to choose from!"

"Give me time, Nurse dear!" said Peridot. "I think . . . I think my hair is too untidy. Will you fetch my ivory brushes?"

Grumbling about her poor old legs the Nurse lumbered up the spiral staircase to the Princess's turret bedroom, and by the time she had lumbered down again and brushed Peridot's pale golden hair till it shone like water, the flower buds had grown to the size of walnuts: but they were tightly closed and there was still no scent.

"Nurse, dear," said Peridot. "Just look at these old shoes I am wearing! Couldn't you fetch me my best pair, the ones with scarlet heels and silver buckles?"

Grumbling still more, the old Nurse set off once again to the Princess's turret bedroom. When she came back with the shoes with scarlet heels and silver buckles, the flower buds were as big as mandarin oranges. But still there was no scent to them.

"Nurse, dear Nurse," said Peridot desperately. "I think with this dress I should be wearing green beads instead of blue . . ."

"Then you can fetch them yourself," said the old Nurse, "for my poor legs will take no more. And you'd best make haste. The fine young princes I saw coming up the stairs didn't look to me as they was used to waiting for anybody. Bless me, what's that?"

As she was speaking the six heart-shaped buds had each burst open one after another with a sound like the plucking of a harp string, and as the petals of each one turned back, the room was filled with the most delicious scent, a mixture of all the flowers that Peridot loved best, of roses and lilac and jasmine and mignonette.

"I think I won't bother about the beads after all, Nurse," said Peridot. "I am ready now!"

And she picked up the flower pot and carrying it before her she went to the Golden Throne Room, and there were six princes standing in a row. That they were all rich she knew, or her father would not have allowed them to present themselves: that they were all handsome she could see. Their trousers were so well pressed that you could have cut your finger on their creases: their shoes were so polished that you could have seen your face in them, and their ties blossomed like the flowers in Peridot's own garden; all except the First Prince. He had very fierce pointed moustaches, and across his chest, pinned to his uniform, was such a row of twinkling medals that Peridot was quite dazzled.

After a great many speeches the King said to her: "Now, my dear, you must choose which of these gallant young men you wish to be your husband."

All the trumpets sounded, and Peridot went up to the First Prince. She curtseyed very low, and breaking off one of the crimson flowers, she held it out to him.

"Pray tell me," she said, "of what does my flower smell?"

The young man took the flower, and after bowing very low he smelt it.

"Of course you can't expect a mere soldier to know much about such things," he said with a puzzled frown. "But it does not smell like a flower at all. Oddly enough, it smells of gunpowder! Not that that is not one of the most delicious smells in the world to me!"

And he went on to talk about the battles he had won, and the towns he had sacked, and the people he had killed, and as he spoke, the flower he was holding drooped, and one by one the crimson petals fell to the floor. It did not need that to show Princess Peridot that this was not the husband she wanted, so she curtseyed again and passed on to the next prince.

"What do you say my flower smells of?" she asked, as she gave him the second crimson blossom.

"Well, flowers are not much in my line, either," said the Second Prince. "It's very odd, but it seems to me it smells of petrol! And what's more, the very kind I use for all the royal cars. I do assure you, ma'am, that if you marry me you will have a fleet of the fastest cars in the world!" And he went on to talk of miles to the gallon, of gaskets, of carburettors and big ends, and long before he had finished the crimson flower had dropped, and its petals drifted to the floor, and Peridot knew that he too was not the right husband.

The Third Prince was rather fat, and down the front of his elegant waistcoat there were one or two gravy stains. He thought the flower smelt of roast beef: the Fourth, who was tall and languid, with crimped and curled hair flowing to his shoulders, thought it smelt of his favourite hair oil. The Fifth, whose suit was brightly checkered, and who wore a golden horse-shoe in his tie, thought it smelt of stables, and with each one of them, the flower dropped and dropped its crimson petals as he held it.

There was nothing outstanding about the last Prince. He was clean shaven and his hair was an ordinary length. His clothes were neat but not unusual. He bowed gravely to Princess Peridot as she curtseyed, and took the sixth flower and studied it for a moment before putting it to his nose.

"In all my palace gardens, which I tend myself, I have never seen a flower like this," he said. "It has the most delicious scent, which seems to be a mixture of all my favourite flowers: the smell of roses, of lilac, of jasmine and of mignonette!"

And the Sixth Prince put the flower in his buttonhole, where its crimson petals went on glowing, if possible more brightly than ever, and Peridot knew without any doubt at all that this was the right husband for her.

"Roses and jasmine indeed! It smelt of gunpowder!" said the First Prince angrily.

"Rubbish! It smelt of petrol!" said the Second Prince.

"Bunkum! Roast beef!" said the Third.

"Hair oil!" said the Fourth.

"Stables!" said the Fifth.

But Princess Peridot and the Sixth Prince, whose name was Benedict, left them to argue it out between them. *They* knew that the crimson flower smelt of roses, lilac, jasmine and mignonette. In no time at all they were married, and the flags flew, and the bells rang till the bell-ropes wore out. There was a wedding cake as tall as a house in the market square, with second helpings for anyone who liked to ask for them, and everyone enjoyed themselves more than ever before: but the people who enjoyed it most of all were Prince Benedict and his bride Peridot.

Simon and the Unicorn

SIMON was kneeling by the lake in the park when he saw the Unicorn. It was closing time, and very faintly he could hear the distant cry, "All out! All out!" of the park keeper, and the ringing of the warning bell, before the gates were closed for the night. He looked forward to this brief moment, whenever he could manage it, when the chattering crowds had gone, and suddenly the park seemed different, silent and mysterious; a place where strange things could happen. He liked to pretend that he was alone in wide, wild country, instead of a public park in a busy city. He had done it so often that he knew exactly how long he could allow between the first "All out!" and a dash to the gates before they were closed with a clang.

Simon was lucky enough to live in a house which, though small and shabby, backed on to the park, and it was from his own bedroom window he had first noticed the strange change that seemed to come over it when the crowds had gone home, and the shadows lengthened.

This particular evening he was kneeling beneath an overhanging bush. The faint, enclosing hum of the distant traffic only served to emphasise the silence round him. He still had a couple of minutes to spare, for he was a fast runner. The darkening wood, which half circled the lake, seemed brooding on goodness-knows-what mysterious secrets. He had just seen a fish rise, and the air was so still that he heard the faint "plop" it made as it fell back into the water, which was as smooth and steely grey as the little old spotted mirror in his bedroom. He turned his head sharply as he heard a twig snap – and there was the Unicorn, glimmering white against the dark trees from which it had come. At first he thought it was a horse that had somehow strayed into the park, but as it came nearer, stepping delicately on shining hooves towards the water, he saw the single, silver horn growing from the centre of its forehead, twisted like a stick of barley sugar, with strange fires flickering in its heart, and he knew at once what it was.

Simon, who had hidden under the bush from a possible park keeper, was also hidden from the Unicorn. So close was he that when the animal stooped to drink, he could see the little eddies of muddy water swirling round its slender fetlocks, and the widening ripples round its soft muzzle as it drank. But at that moment he heard, far away, the last "All out!". So distant was it that it might have been the cry of some strange bird, but he knew he must go at once.

At the first rustle of leaves as he crept from his hiding place, the Unicorn threw up its head in alarm, scattering silver drops with the tips of its upflung mane. It stamped with its forefeet in

the shallow water, with a rush of bubbles, turned and galloped
back to the shelter of the little wood, its long tail, tufted like a
lion's, streaming behind, and vanished among the trees. If it had
not been for the rocking of the lily pads on the lake, Simon would
have thought he had dreamed it all.

But he had no time to stand and wonder. When he panted up
to the park gates the keeper was just that moment turning the
key in the lock. When he saw Simon he twisted the key back
again and pretended to give him a cuff as he went through, for
he knew this game of Simon's well. Simon grinned, dodged the
cuff and ran home.

*   *   *

"You couldn't have seen a Unicorn, because there aren't such
things!" said George and Henry when he told them at school in
the playground next morning.

At once Simon was sorry he had said anything about it. But
having told them, it seemed absolutely necessary that he should
make them believe him. Henry was a pale shadow of George
and always agreed with him.

"Just supposing it was true, and old Sim wasn't pulling our
legs, what a lark if we could catch his blessed Unicorn!" said
George. "But of course there isn't such a thing. I've never seen
one, anyway."

"Well, it *is* true!" said Simon hotly. "You've never seen a
rhinoceros, but that doesn't mean there isn't such a creature!"

"Well then, if you're so jolly sure, let's try and catch it," said
George.

"Yes, let's!" said Henry.

Simon knew that to capture such a splendid creature was a
hateful idea, but at that moment the urge to make the two boys
believe him seemed even more important.

"All right then, we will," he said angrily. Then remembering
the needle-point of the wonderful horn, and the sharp hoof
prints in the mud, he went on uneasily: "But how shall we do it?"

"Easy," said Henry. "You make a beautiful maiden sit down in one of its favourite haunts, and it lies down and puts its head in her lap – and then the hunters take it prisoner."

"However do you know that?" asked George curiously.

Henry blushed a rosy red and said uncomfortably, "Read it somewhere." He was not a boy who was given to much reading.

Of course we aren't hunters, thought Simon. If we did catch it, we should let it go again. It wouldn't do any harm just to try. Then he said, "But we don't know any beautiful maidens."

"There's Mavis Budge in our class," said George. "She's not bad looking."

"I think Maureen is prettier," said Henry. "Couldn't we ask them both? Then Sim's Unicorn could take its choice!"

George agreed to this, and the two of them laughed as though it was the funniest joke in the world, and Simon wished more than ever that he had said nothing about it. Not only were George and Henry taking over what had been his own splendid discovery, but now two giggling girls were to be let into the secret; but it was too late to go back.

Mavis and Maureen were perfectly willing to be considered rival beautiful maidens, for each was convinced that she would be chosen. They agreed to meet the two boys at the park entrance half an hour before closing time.

As luck would have it, Simon's mother was going out that evening, and she told him he must take his young sister Lucy with him. When they met at the gate Mavis was wearing her best mauve frock with the frills round the edge. Maureen's hair was still in curlers. She was leaving them in until the last minute, she said, and would take them out when she was sitting down and waiting for the Unicorn. Both girls looked scornfully at Lucy, who was a mousy little person with spectacles, and a slight stammer.

"It's all right," said Simon. "I've told Lucy what's happening and she's promised not to be a nuisance. Now don't forget we've only got until the last 'All out!' for the whole thing to happen.

That's not more than twenty minutes. When I say 'Run for it!', make for the gates for all you are worth. We don't want to be locked in the park all night."

They reached the lake in plenty of time. The sun had gone in and a chilly little breeze had sprung up, so that the few people who were there were already drifting homewards. The two girls sat down on the grassy bank a few feet apart. Mavis spread a comic paper to sit on so that she should not stain the mauve dress, Maureen took out her curlers so that the newly released hair stuck out in ringlets as tight as bed springs. No one took any notice of Lucy, who settled herself a little way off, humming quietly as she made a daisy chain with the flowers she had picked in the grass as they came along.

When the first "All out!" sounded, the three boys stopped talking and crouched out of sight among the bushes at the edge of the lake. They waited in silence. At first nothing happened, and George said scornfully, "I knew all the time Sim was just pretending! There isn't such a thing as . . ."

"Shut up!" hissed Simon. "Look there!"

It was the Unicorn. It came towards them from the little wood, slowly this time. It was limping, and as it drew near they could see it was leaving behind a trail of drops of blood; but its magnificent head was held high, and the lights in its great horn flickered strangely.

"Gosh, it's true after all!" whispered George.

"It's hurt!" Simon whispered back. "Cut its foot on a broken bottle in the grass, I shouldn't wonder."

"All the easier to catch it!" answered George.

Mavis looked a little nervously over her shoulder, then she arranged herself and the frilly frock in a position she had seen in a dress advertisement. She put on the smile she used when she was having her photograph taken and waited. For a brief moment the Unicorn paused beside her, then it tossed its head, almost it seemed in derision, and limped on to where Maureen, open-mouthed, curls bouncing, edged nervously back. Again the

Unicorn paused, pawed the ground with one silver hoof, whinnied in disdain, tossed its splendid head, and limped on once more.

"Well, I'm blowed!" began Henry.

"Shut up!" said Simon again. "Look at it now!"

The Unicorn had raised its muzzle and was sniffing the air, and then it saw Lucy. She was sitting on the grass, still humming to herself and making the daisy chain. She had taken off her spectacles and put them in her pocket, because they were new and were making the bridge of her nose sore, and she had lost her hair ribbon, so that instead of wearing her hair scraped back as usual, it hung in two bright wings on either side of her face. She looked up and smiled at the Unicorn without a trace of fear, and the great animal lowered its head as if in homage and knelt before her. Then it lay down, putting its head in the lap of her faded blue frock.

"I think it's a silly, soppy game!" said Mavis, bursting into tears of vexation.

"So do I!" said Maureen, stamping her foot. "I'm going home

this instant minute!" And the two girls ran away together as a yet more distant "All out!" sounded.

Simon, George and Henry came cautiously from their hiding place to where the Unicorn lay. Lucy was stroking its soft muzzle, seeming not in the least afraid.

"Then it's true!" said George again. "Boy, oh boy!"

"Of course it's true," said Simon. "So now we've proved it we can let it go again."

"Let it go?" said George. "Not on your life! Let's hide it somewhere and charge people a bob a go to have a squint at it!"

George planned to be a successful businessman one day. He had already practised writing his signature very large, and with so many flourishes that no one could read it, which he said was necessary for signing important letters.

"My book says a Unicorn's horn makes poisoned food good to eat," said Henry. "Queen Elizabeth the First had a little cup made of one."

"We might cut off its horn and sell it in tiny little bits, and make hundreds of pounds!" said George.

"But . . . but who has poisoned food nowadays?" said Simon. He was horrified at the idea, but it was all he could think of saying.

"You never know what's in school dinners!" said Henry darkly. "Peter Parsons was sick the other day."

"But you can't do anything so utterly beastly to my Unicorn!" said Simon.

"It isn't your Unicorn now," said George. "It's ours as well, Henry's and mine, so it's two against one."

"That's right," said Henry.

"I tell you, we can make our fortunes!" went on George. "If you make a fuss, Sim, we shall tell the park keeper about it, and then your precious Unicorn will be put in a zoo, or a circus or something. Why shouldn't we get the benefit from it?"

Simon was just about to explode with anger when Lucy said quietly, without the trace of a stammer:

"Until its hurt foot is healed we can't do anything with it.

It needs proper bathing and bandaging. Till then we shall have to keep it somewhere safely hidden."

The three boys turned and looked at her in astonishment. She had tied her handkerchief round the injured foot, but blood was already oozing through.

Simon was the most surprised of the three. He stared at his sister, and he found himself looking at her properly for the first time, as far as a brother can. He suddenly realised that she was not bad to look at, after all. Perhaps, he thought, the scraped-back hair, and the spectacles, and the spots she sometimes had, were just the growing pains of being beautiful. But the fact that mousy little Lucy, who would not usually say "Boo" to a goose, had just spoken out so firmly and sensibly had struck all three boys dumb. Simon broke the astonished silence.

"I say," he said. "The last 'All out!' went ages ago, and the bell has stopped ringing. We're locked in the park!"

George let out a slow whistle, and at once their differences were forgotten.

"They'd let us out if we knocked up the park keeper," said Henry uneasily.

"What, and say we were so busy catching a unicorn that we missed the 'All out!'? Not likely," said George. "They'd think we'd gone potty, unless we showed it to them, and that's the last thing we want because then they'd be certain to take it away."

"It's quite simple," said Lucy, and there was still no trace of a stammer. "We can hide it in the old hen house at the bottom of our yard. It hasn't been used for hens for ages."

"And how shall we get it there when the gate is locked?" said George. "Fly, I suppose!" he added scornfully.

"Someone can make a 'back' so that the others can get over our fence, where it runs along the edge of the park," said Lucy.

"And what about the one who makes the 'back'? He'll be left behind with the Unicorn. It won't be me, for certain!" said George. "I'm not going to be left alone with it!"

"Nor me!" said Henry.

"The ones who get over first must make a hole in the fence so that I can lead the Unicorn through into the yard," said Lucy.

"Why should you lead it?" said George, who wished he had thought of all this himself, and who felt his usual role of cock of the gang slipping, and that to a girl. "*I* shall lead it."

As he spoke he made "come up" noises to the Unicorn, and tweeked its mane. But the animal raised its head, bared its teeth, and lashed out with its uninjured leg. It caught George a glancing blow on his shin.

"Ow! That hurt!" he said, and added sulkily, "Oh, all right. You can lead it if you like, Lucy."

"I think it will do what I ask," she said quietly. She patted the creature's sleek neck and whispered something in its ear, and at once the Unicorn stood up. The three boys watched in astonishment as she looped the daisy chain round its unresisting neck, and led it away at a pace to suit its limping progress. In the gathering dusk, the strange fires burning in the great horn cast a faint radiance about the two of them. In a slightly awed silence the three boys followed.

Luckily there was no one at home when Simon and George climbed in turn on to Henry's bent back, and scrambled over the fence into the yard behind; and no one to hear the splintering of wood as they pulled away three boards to make room for Lucy and the Unicorn to pass through. When she had bathed the wounded fetlock, which had an ugly gash, and had bound it up with cooling ointment and clean bandage, for it would allow no one else to come near, persuaded by Lucy the Unicorn seemed quite content to lie down among the odds and ends which were stored in the shed. If any of the boys tried to touch it, it would struggle to its feet, baring its teeth and tossing its splendid head, so that the tapering horn made a shining arc in the dark little shed.

"Better wait until its hoof is better before we try to show it off," said George. "P'raps it won't be in such a beastly temper then."

Lucy nodded. "We'd much better wait," she said.

"We might even charge ten pence a time for a squint. It's worth it," went on George from a safe distance. "Time we were going, Henry. So long, Sim! See you to-morrow."

They went, rattling a stick along the railings as they ran down the road.

Lucy locked the hen house door behind them and put the key in her pocket.

"Whatever's come over you?" said Simon. "It's a perfectly horrible idea to lock up the Unicorn and make people pay to gawp at it!"

"Of course it is," said Lucy quietly. "No one is going to if I can help it."

"But George and Henry . . . ?" began Simon.

"Leave it to me," said this new, confident Lucy. "I've got a different plan. I locked the door to keep people out, not the Unicorn in. As soon as its foot is well enough for it to fend for itself, and the park is empty of people, we'll let it go. There's Mum calling. We'd better go in."

And to Simon's surprise he found himself doing what his sister told him.

The next day when George and Henry came to see the Unicorn, George said, "It's a funny thing, but it isn't half so smashing as I thought last night. Better only charge five pence, after all."

It was true. Its coat, which had gleamed so silvery white the evening before, looked dull and lack-lustre.

"It won't eat anything," said Simon in distress. "Not grass, or oats even. We found a packet in the store cupboard. And it won't drink anything either. We tried it with our breakfast milk when it wouldn't drink water. Just lies there with its head in Lucy's lap."

"My book says Unicorns would rather die than live in captivity," said Henry.

"Then we must let it go at once!" said Simon.

"What, with the park full of people?" said George. "They'd

only capture it instead of us. Besides, what about all that money it's going to earn us? Walk up! Walk up! Come and see the only living Unicorn in captivity! . . . I tell you, I can almost hear those pence jingling!"

The second day the Unicorn's fetlock was a little better, but it stood with hanging head, its mane, once so glossy white, hung dull and lifeless, a common grey.

"It's not much to look at after all," said George. "Can't think why we were so stuck on it at first. I doubt if we could ask more than two and a half pence a look. Even its horn is not shining so much."

It was true. The fires that burned in the wonderful horn that had glowed now blue, now green, flickered uncertainly.

The third day the fires in the Unicorn's horn had smouldered so low and it hung its head so dejectedly that George said, "I vote we get some of Class IV to come along to-morrow to have a look at it. It's too late this evening. We may as well make a little money out of it in case . . . It doesn't look long for this world. Better only ask a penny a peep, after all. What do you think, Henry?"

And Henry, of course, agreed. The two boys sauntered off.

Lucy was examining the wounded heel, and the "All out!" was drifting over the fence.

"Couldn't we let it go *now*, Lucy?" asked Simon in desperate anxiety.

"It's better, but it isn't quite well enough," said Lucy.

"But George is bringing half the class to see it to-morrow morning. One of them is sure to blab about it, and George is right. Once grown-ups know we've captured a real Unicorn they'll keep it prisoner for always. That would be horrible! What on earth can we do?"

"Keep the door locked and lose the key," said Lucy calmly. "Before school no one will have time to do much about it. That will give us a little longer still for the cut to heal."

But as things turned out they did not have to lose the key.

In the middle of the night Simon was woken by a strange noise. It sounded like someone hammering in the yard. But who would hammer in the middle of the night? He slipped out of bed and ran to the window. The sound seemed to be coming from the old hen house.

"I do believe it's the Unicorn trying to get out!" said Simon to himself. "If it can beat on the door like that it must be feeling well enough to go free!"

The moon was full, and its pale magic lit up the park over the fence as brightly as day, but the shadows in the little yard below were black as pitch. As he looked, the Unicorn redoubled its battering on the door. Someone must stop it or it would wake his parents. Simon was putting on his slippers, trying not to think how the creature might rear up with lashing hooves as he opened the door, when his sharp ears heard the familiar sound of the bolts on the back door being shot back, very quietly. He ran to the window again, and was just in time to see Lucy, barefoot and in her nightgown, run across the yard with the key of the door in her hand. He had forgotten that she kept it under her pillow. She unlocked the door of the shed and stood on one side, and the Unicorn, head erect, the strange fires leaping in its horn once more, stepped into the moonlight. It was no longer limping. It threw back its head and snuffed the night air as Lucy, with some difficulty, pulled away the planks of the fence which had been removed before, and never properly replaced. And the Unicorn bent its proud head and stepped delicately into the moonlit park. It paused for a moment and looked back. Lucy ran up to the great animal, and standing on tiptoe put her arms around its gleaming neck. It nuzzled her shoulder for a moment, and then she let go, and the creature tossed its silver mane in the moonlight, kicked up its heels for joy at its freedom, and galloped away. Lucy stood and watched until it disappeared in the shadows of the wood. The glow of its horn flickered briefly between the tree trunks, and it was gone. She gave a great sigh, and padded across the yard on her bare feet back to bed.

The anger of George and Henry knew no bounds next morning when they heard what she had done. But there was nothing they could do about it.

"Like your blooming cheek, young Lucy, letting our Unicorn go!" said George furiously. "Anyone would think it was yours, the way you go on!"

"It wasn't mine," she said gravely. "Just because we locked it up it didn't make it belong to any of us. It belonged to itself."

"Never mind," said Henry. "P'raps it will come back again. You never know."

But it never did, although they watched for several evenings.

And Lucy? From that day she never stammered again, and though she continued to be a quiet little person, no one would ever call her mousy now.

Minching and Munching Mouseling

THERE was once a little Munching Mouseling. He lived in a hole
in a corner of a carpenter's workshop, and very snug it was too.
All safe and sound from cats and traps, with a soft bed of sawdust
to sleep on, and a curl of wood shavings to keep out the draught.
The carpenter was glad of Mouseling's company. They talked
together of this and that, and when the little creature was in a
cheerful mood, he would dance a gay fandango to the tap, tap,
tap of the old man's hammer.

One day Munching Mouseling said:

"I am sorry to say that I must leave you, my friend, for to-
morrow I am to be married to my cousin Miss Minching Mouseling."

"Married? My poor fellow!" said the carpenter, who was a
bachelor himself, with a poor opinion of women. "But even so,
I see no reason why you should go away."

"My Minching says your hole would be too small. Besides,
she has set her dear little heart on a very superior hole in Mrs
Bobbin's shop, the draper's round the corner. I have already

furnished it with an empty cotton reel for a table, and two plastic thimbles to sit upon."

"Huh!" grumbled the old man. "Too grand for a hole in a carpenter's workshop! Now your troubles will begin, young Mouseling!"

"Perhaps my Minching is a little . . . particular," said the mouse. "But her eyes are so bright, and her whiskers so silky, that nothing in the world is too good for her!"

Next day Munching Mouseling married his Minching, and they went to live in the mouse hole under the counter of Mrs Bobbin's shop.

"Not *one* of my friends lives in a hole in a draper's shop!" said Minching proudly. "Or sits on a thimble at a cotton reel table! How happy I am in my new home!"

And so she was: but not for long.

Mrs Bobbin dropped so very few crumbs from her lunchtime sandwich, and these were so very small, that unless the two mice were careful, they all fell down the hole in the middle of the cotton reel table and were lost.

"I don't think I like living in a draper's shop after all," said Minching at last. "At home there was always plenty to eat, but here – why, I am growing quite thin! My father the grocer would be shocked to hear how hungry I am." (You must know that every mouse is called by the trade of the owner of the house in which he has his hole, and Minching's father lived in a grocer's shop.) "I have set my heart on living in a supermarket!" she went on. "There, I'm told, you simply help yourself to any food that takes your fancy, and put it in a trolley and wheel it away!"

"Very well, my dear," said Munching. "Nothing is too good for my lovely Minching. But we haven't got a trolley."

"Then make one!" said Minching sharply.

So Munching made a little trolley from the tray of a match box, with four buttons for wheels and a pipe cleaner for a handle. It squeaked a little when they pushed it, and it didn't run very smoothly, for the buttons were not quite the same size. "But it will be so useful for moving house!" said Minching, as they loaded it with the two thimbles. The cotton reel was too big, so it had to be left behind.

They could not find a mouse hole in the supermarket, it was much too new for that. But Munching discovered a dark little corner under a pile of cardboard boxes which they thought would do just as well. "How proud I am to be the first mouse to live in a supermarket!" said Minching, as she trundled her trolley round, taking a lump of sugar here and a broken biscuit there. "How happy I am in my new home!"

And so she was: but not for long.

There was plenty of food on the shelves, but so much of it was in tins; and the supermarket seemed so full of human feet. There were feet in high heels and feet in low heels, and feet in black boots and red boots and brown boots, so that Minching and Munching were for ever dodging for fear they should be squashed as flat as pancakes.

One day when Minching had gone out alone with the trolley, to find "a little something tasty for supper," she did not come back. Munching went up and down the aisles calling sadly for her, but what with the trampling of many feet and the clatter of the tills, no one heard. When the supermarket was closed for the night and empty of people, he found her at last among the frozen vegetables, frozen too, cold and stiff as a fish finger, with a single pea clutched tightly in her paws.

"Minching! Minching! Speak to me, Minching!" cried Munching. But she answered never a word.

With the greatest difficulty Munching lifted her down and thawed her out on the hot water pipes. As soon as she could speak she twittered:

"Oh my! Oh my! What a terrible thing to happen! Frozen stiff as a fish finger! Not to mention being nearly squashed as flat as a pancake a hundred times a day! I can't live in a supermarket one moment longer, it's far too dangerous! What would

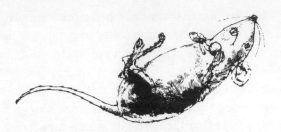

my aunt the headmistress say? I tell you what, Munching my love,
I think I should like to live in a school!"

"Very well, my dear," said Munching. "Nothing is too good
for my lovely Minching!"

They loaded up the trolley with the two thimbles and the
frozen pea and trundled off, squeaketty-squeak, to the nearest
school. There they made their home in the toe of a Wellington
boot in the Lost Property cupboard, and very snug it was too.

"None of my friends have a home in a Lost Property cupboard
in the toe of a Wellington boot!" said Minching proudly as she
nibbled away at one of the carrot tops which had been put to
grow in a saucer of water on the Nature Table. "How happy I
am in my new home!"

And so she was: but not for long.

Soon they had finished all there was to eat on the Nature Table:
the carrot tops: the beans growing in blotting paper: the mustard
and cress on flannel, and they had to go further afield for food.
Minching found a milk bottle which someone had left in a corner
of the classroom. She was balancing on the rim, peering inside,
and wondering how she could reach the little puddle of milk
at the bottom, when she heard a noise, and when she looked up
what should she see but the Caretaker's Cat grinning down at
her, and purring wickedly, like a squadron of aeroplanes!
Minching was so frightened that she lost her balance and fell,
plop! right inside the milk bottle! At the same time the Cat made
a pounce, the bottle overturned with a clatter and went rolling
across the floor, luckily towards the open door of the Lost
Property cupboard.

Munching looked up from the teacher's desk where he was busy trying the taste of a pot of paste, and leaped gallantly to her rescue.

"Run for it, Minching!" he called. And giddy with rolling and draggled with milk, as the bottle hit the cupboard she squeezed herself out and dived for the safety of the Wellington boot. Munching was just in time to slam the door behind them in the face of the grinning Cat.

"Oh my! Oh my!" twittered Minching. "What a terrible thing to happen! I can't stay in a school a minute longer! Frightened out of my wits by the Caretaker's Cat, and half drowned in a bottle of milk! What would my uncle the Archdeacon say? I tell you what, Munching my love, I think I should like to go and live in the cathedral!" (A cathedral, as you know, is a grand kind of church.)

Munching sighed, but he said:

"Very well, my dear. I *still* say nothing is too good for my lovely Minching!"

So they loaded the trolley with the two thimbles, the frozen pea, and a piece of chalk, which Minching was certain would be good to eat if she only knew how to cook it. When the Caretaker's Cat grew tired of waiting outside the cupboard door and went away, they trundled the trolley, squeaketty-squeak, out of the classroom, across the playground, and down the road.

"Of course, my dear, it will be very grand to live in a cathedral," said Munching doubtfully. "But I don't think we shall find very much to eat there."

But he was wrong. It was Harvest Festival, and besides the vases of flowers, glowing as brightly as the stained glass windows, there were piles of fruit and vegetables on every ledge and in every corner. There were carrots and onions and vegetable marrows; and apples and pears and tomatoes; and loaves of bread made in the shape of sheaves of corn, and Minching and Munching stuffed and stuffed, so that they became so fat they had to make the mouse hole they had nibbled in one of the hassocks much bigger. They garaged the trolley underneath a prayer book that had fallen on the floor with the spine uppermost.

"None of my friends have ever had a mouse hole in a cathedral!" said Minching, as grandly as she was able with her mouth full of banana. "How happy I am in my new home!"

And so she was: but not for long.

The very next day, which was Sunday, there was a deep rumbling from the organ, and the clatter of many feet walking up the aisle, and without any warning at all a great six-foot human being knelt on the hassock in which Munching and Minching had nibbled their home! They only just had time to escape before the roof fell in. One of the thimbles was crushed to little pieces.

"Oh my! Oh my!" twittered Minching. "What a thing to happen! I can't stay another minute in a cathedral. Nearly knelt on by a great clumsy human! What would my great-aunt the Queen say!" (Minching's great-aunt lived in a mouse hole in the lowest kitchen of one of the royal houses.) "And now I think of it," she went on, "I should like to live in Buckingham Palace!"

"Buckingham Palace!" said Munching, aghast.

"Well, you always said that nothing was too good for your lovely Minching," she said sulkily.

"Very well, my dear," said Munching with a sigh.

So they loaded up the trolley once more with the remaining thimble, the frozen pea, the piece of chalk and a juicy grape they had stolen from the pulpit. Squeaketty-squeak they went down the aisle – luckily everyone was singing a hymn, so nobody heard them – squeaketty-squeak along one street after another, until they came at last to Buckingham Palace. Past the sentries at the great gates they went, squeaketty-squeak across the courtyard, through the front door and rather nervously up the red-carpeted stairs, with a guardsman standing with drawn sword on every one. They hurried along a wide corridor, until at last they came to a great room, with the Queen herself sitting on her golden throne at the far end. Munching Mouseling was trembling in every limb, but Minching said grandly:

"I wish to live underneath the throne itself!"

It was draughty underneath the throne, and the marble was very cold. Not at all what Munching called "homey". But Minching puffed herself out with pride and said between chattering teeth:

"I am the grandest mouse in the world! Not one of my friends has ever lived under the throne in Buckingham Palace! How delighted I am with my new home!"

At that very minute a round diamond button came off the Queen's gown. It fell on the floor and rolled under the throne.

"And none of my friends has a round diamond button to use as a ball!" went on Minching.

"But, my dear!" said Munching. "Suppose the Queen wants her diamond back again? Besides, it may be a very important button!"

"If she wants it, she must ask for it!" said Minching in her grandest voice. "And ask me *nicely*!"

As she spoke, the Queen, who had already missed her diamond button, called to her Guards to look for it. They searched and searched. They tramped with their great boots, and poked with their sharp swords, but they could not find the diamond button. At last one of them went down on his hands and knees and felt with his sword, swish! swish! underneath the throne. If Minching and Munching had not jumped over the first swish, why, they would have had their feet cut off! And if they had not ducked beneath the second swish, they would both have lost their heads!

"Oh my! Oh my!" twittered Minching breathlessly. "What a terrible thing to happen!"

But Munching said:

"I don't care how much you like your new home! From now on we are going to live in a mouse hole of *my* choosing!"

And he loaded up the trolley with the thimble, the frozen pea,

the piece of chalk, the juicy grape, and, I am sorry to say, the diamond button, and they pushed it from under the throne. Bouncetty-bounce they went down the marble steps. Now the Queen has very sharp eyes and very sharp ears, and she heard them go squeaketty-squeak down the room, and she saw the diamond button twinkle. She pointed with her sceptre and called to her Guards:

"Stop those mice!"

Minching and Munching only ran the faster, with the Guards pounding after them in their great boots and calling: "Stop! Stop, thief!"

Down the steps bumped Minching and Munching. Squeaketty-squeak across the courtyard they went. And just as they reached the sentry at the great gates, the diamond button bounced out of the trolley and rolled to his feet, and he ran to the Palace to tell the Queen. On hurried Minching and Munching, squeaketty-squeak into the street. They ran and ran, and next the juicy grape fell out, and then the piece of chalk, followed at last by the frozen pea; and just as they turned into the street where the carpenter lived, the thimble bounced out and rolled away, and Munching did not stop to pick up one of them. He did not slacken speed until he was right inside the carpenter's workshop. The old man was at his hammering, just as before, and he peered at Minching and Munching over his spectacles, and said:

"So it's you again, young feller! I thought you might be back, so I've kept your mouse hole aired for you, and very pleased I am to see you again. No doubt I shall get used to your wife in time!"

So Minching and Munching dived into the old mouse hole, and Munching gave a great sigh of relief, and at least Minching did not say a word of complaint.

The very next day she presented her Munching with six little pink baby miceling, and said:

"My dear, how glad I am to be in such a splendid place for bringing up a family. How clever of you to find it! So safe from cats and traps, with a soft sawdust bed to sleep on and a curl of wood shavings to keep out the draught!"

"I am glad you are pleased, my love," said Munching. "But shall we not now need a perambulator?"

"Not at all, my dear," said Minching. "The trolley will do very well instead!"

Parradiddle Pete

ONCE upon a time a young woman was coming home from
market, humming cheerfully to herself because she knew that
her man would say "Well done!" when she reached their cottage
on the other side of Dundreary Moor, for she had sold all her

eggs and butter at a fine price. Her baby slept peacefully, slung on her back, and the welcome money jingled pleasantly in her pocket. The basket hung lightly on her arm, empty now of everything except for a bit of bread and cheese wrapped up in a napkin, which she had brought for her dinner. Although it was evening she had been far too busy to eat so much as a mouthful.

"And it will be even lighter by the weight of the bread and cheese," she said to herself, "just as soon as I can turn off the road and find a comfortable spot to sit and take off my Sunday shoes. For truth to tell, though they look so fine, they're fairly killing me."

She waited until she had gone a mile or two across the moor, for her pride would not let her go barefoot, to which she was much more accustomed, until there was no chance of being overtaken by any of the smart town people who had been at the market.

When she could see that the road was empty, both behind and before, she turned off its stony surface, and finding a little grassy place among the heather she sat herself down, with the baby sleeping beside her, and her back against a boulder. With a sigh of relief she kicked off her shoes.

She was wriggling her toes with pleasure at the freedom of them, and getting down to a mouthful of food, when she heard a little tapping sound. At first she thought it was a blackbird pecking at a snail shell. But no bird would peck with so constant a rhythm, however juicy the snail. "Pim-pam-parradiddle" went the little tapping noise, over and over again. Nancy, for that was her name, looked about her, with her mouth full of bread and cheese, for the tapping noise seemed to be coming nearer, and there, marching through the heather, she saw a little man no bigger than her milking pail, beating away with a pair of little sticks, on a drum at his side no bigger than a teacup! "Pim-pam-parradiddle" he went, his drumsticks rattling so fast they seemed nothing but a blur.

When he drew level with Nancy, he tossed his sticks into the air, and caught them neatly as they came twirling down again, and beat his little drum once more with a shower of taps, all woven round his "pim-pam-parradiddle" so that she sat open-mouthed with astonishment at his skill.

When he had done, he whipped off his cap with the owl's feather in it, and bowed low before her, and at the same time she noticed that the tips of the pointed ears that stuck through his straw-coloured hair, and the tips of his long fingers, were both as green as lettuce leaves.

"Can you spare a crumb or two of your bread and cheese to a poor drummer?" asked the little man in a wheedling voice, which was light but musical as water running from a waterspout.

He looked such a poor thin little thing, with his ragged clothes flapping round him, that Nancy felt pity for him, as she did for her own child when he was hungry; and though she was hungry herself, she said:

"Why, take it all and welcome."

And she handed him the two hunks of brown bread with the golden cheese clapped in the middle.

The little man sat down cross-legged before her, and holding the sandwich with both hands made short work of it; though how such a large piece of food could disappear inside a little thing no bigger than a skinned rabbit, and show no bulge or bump she couldn't imagine.

Now while the little man was munching away the baby awoke and began to cry, and do what she would, Nancy could not quieten him.

"Hush, hush now, my little Peter!" she crooned, rocking him in her arms. But he would not be comforted.

"It's his teeth he's cutting," said she, and explained to the little man that she had dropped his teething ring at the market.

The little man stared at the baby with slanting, unblinking eyes and said:

"Why human children can't be born complete I've always wondered. But if it's something hard to bite on he wants, he won't find anything harder than this, so I'll make him a present of it."

As he spoke, he put one of his drumsticks in the baby's fat fist, and little Peter put one end in his mouth, stopped crying at once and bit on it contentedly.

"But can you drum with only one stick?" asked Nancy.

"There are plenty more where that came from, my dear," said the little man.

And taking a knife from his pocket he cut a straight bit of heather, and trimmed and smoothed it, and although it had none of the curious carving of the one the baby was chumbling, in no time at all there was another drumstick just as serviceable. To prove it, he jumped to his feet and began such a shower of drum taps that Nancy could hardly see the sticks at all. The tapping they made, now loud, now soft, sounded sometimes like the patter of hundreds of tiny dancing feet, sometimes like the soft beat of raindrops on the sun-parched earth, sometimes like the harsh rattle of hailstones on the window pane; but always it was woven round the rhythm of the "pim-pam-parradiddle" she had heard at first. And the baby laughed with glee and jiggled his feet, and waved his drumstick in the air: and the little man laughed with him, harsh as the cry of a cock pheasant.

Then he said:

"You've been kind to me, Nancy my dear, so I'll do what I can to repay you. What would you like for your baby here in the future, Fame or Fortune? Think carefully now!"

Nancy thought and thought, and at last she said, "If I say Fortune, he might turn extravagant, and end up as poor as his daddy. I think I'd rather it was Fame, if you please."

The little man nodded.

"Then Fame it shall be," he said. "In the meantime, take care of the drumstick, my dear, and good day to you."

So saying he lifted his tattered cap to her, stuck it on again at a jaunty angle and marched away through the heather, his little drum bouncing on his thigh, as once again he played his "pim-pam-parradiddle". Nancy watched him grow smaller and smaller, and heard the drumming grow fainter and fainter, until he disappeared down what she had thought was a rabbit hole.

It was only when she got up to go that she noticed that she had been sitting in the middle of a fairy ring: one of those circles of grass of darker green which show where the Little People have been dancing.

"So that's how it was that I could see him!" she said to herself, and she gathered up the baby who had dropped contentedly off to sleep again, and set off for home on her bare feet, with her Sunday shoes wrapped up in the napkin in her basket.

Now Nancy told her husband nothing of her strange meeting with the little man, in case he should say she had made the wrong choice, for they were very poor indeed. Neither did she tell Peter, even when he was old enough to understand, in case knowing he would one day be famous should make him proud. But she let him have the fairy drumstick, and told him always to take care of it, for one day it would bring him good luck. One curious thing she noticed was that as he grew up, whenever he made a tapping noise, however idly, whether it was with his spoon on his little cracked baby plate, or when he knocked upon his rich uncle's knocker, or even when drumming idly with his fingers on the table, sooner or later, however he started, his tapping turned into the "pim-pam-parradiddle" of the fairy drummer, so that he came to be known round about as Parradiddle Pete.

When he was fifteen he had grown into a tall, pleasant-faced boy: but there was no sign of either Fame or Fortune. And then one day a Recruiting Sergeant came to the village, with his soldiers in their red coats, and a great deal of noise and beer and excitement. When Peter saw the brave scarlet and heard the drum beating its "tuck-tucka-tuck", he said to the Recruiting Sergeant:

"If you please, your honour, if I enlist in the King's army, do you think I might learn to be a drummer boy?"

The Sergeant, who rather liked being called "your honour" and whose job it was to be pleasant – until he'd got his men signed-up and on the parade ground – laughed and said:

"What makes you think you'd be any good at that, my lad? Here, Barney, let's see what he can do!"

And he winked at the soldier with the drum, who grinned, and handed it to Peter who took it, and one of the sticks. Seeing him take the little fairy drumstick from his pocket, to take the place of the second, the crowd began to laugh. And no one laughed more heartily than the Recruiting Sergeant. But as soon as the first uncertain taps settled down into his "pim-pam-parradiddle", they stopped laughing. For the tapping of the two sticks flickered over the tightly-stretched drum skin, as sure and neat as a country dance. It echoed from house to house, so that windows shot up and heads came out to listen, and the toes of the crowd began to tap all round him, to the rhythm of the flying drumsticks. Even the Recruiting Sergeant grinned, and drummed with his fingers on the table. At last, with a final flourish, Peter stopped with his sticks upraised, and looked anxiously round. The crowd laughed and clapped, and the Recruiting Sergeant slapped him on the back so hard that Peter nearly fell over, and said:

"You'll do, you'll do, my lad! Name?"

"Parradiddle Pete," said Peter, and then he remembered that was not his proper name as it was written in the great church register. But when he tried to explain, the Recruiting Sergeant had lost interest, and was already questioning someone else. So Parradiddle Pete he remained, and as no one was allowed to go home to say good-bye, in case they changed their minds and never came back, Peter sént a message to his mother by a neighbour. And she, poor woman, gave a sigh, but like all mothers she knew that these things must happen when children grow up. And Peter marched away to be a soldier with a shilling in his pocket and a ribbon in his hat and high expectations in his heart.

So Parradiddle Pete became a drummer boy. Of course he used two regimental drumsticks, not the fairy one; but he kept it in a pocket of his fine scarlet coat. Sometimes he took it out and fingered the strange carvings on its side, but always he kept it safe because his mother had told him that one day it would bring him luck.

Peter learned the language of the drum with surprising ease, for its drag and flam will carry further than any human voice when all is quiet, and more surely through the deafening sounds of battle, giving heart to the men who fight, into the bargain. But although he was all that a drummer boy should be, and popular with his comrades also, on the rare occasions when he could find someone to pen a letter home (for he could neither read nor write) it seemed to his mother that he was as far from Fame as ever. As for Fortune, a drummer boy earned no more than fourpence a week.

Time went by, and after a couple of years of carefree peace, the rumblings of war were heard, and Peter became a seasoned drummer, no longer on the parade ground now, but with the cries of the wounded and the thunder of the guns filling the air, so that the harsh bray of the trumpets and the sharp repeated rattle of the drums were the only commands that could be heard above the ugly din of battle.

At last it came about that a great fight was to be fought which would decide the whole fortune of the campaign, and the very future of the King himself upon his golden throne. As luck would have it, the field of battle was none other than Dundreary Moor.

The sun was just sucking up the last shreds of night mist when the drummers woke the sleeping soldiers with their harsh repeated rattle. The two armies fought through the heat of the morning and the long, weary afternoon. By evening the high hopes of Peter and his red-coated friends had turned to despair, for the tide of battle had turned against them, and fewer and fewer men were left to return the fire of their green-coated enemies. Peter himself was weak from loss of blood from a sabre cut on his forehead. When the crimson sun was sinking in a bank of dark cloud, ragged as the banners of the armies fighting below, the enemy sounded the "Charge!" with every chance of finishing off their opponents and winning the day. The haggard General of Peter's army, knowing there was no hope, with his men now reduced to a quarter of the brave number who had faced the enemy so gallantly that morning, ordered the Retreat to be beaten.

Peter, who was the only drummer able still to stand, staggered to his feet. One of his drumsticks had splintered when he had fallen, struck down by the sabre cut. Hardly knowing what he did, he took the fairy drumstick from his pocket, tightened the drum skin so that it was taut and firm, and brought down his ill-matched sticks on the goatskin as smartly as he was able. But instead of the "Retreat" which he had meant to beat, the drumsticks seemed to take control. After a few ragged notes it was the "pim-pam-parradiddle" that rose in the air with a surge of flying taps. Louder and louder they sounded, over and over again, and new hope rose within the men with the remorseless sound; new strength seemed to rise in their limbs. The wounded shook off their despair, picked up their weapons again and stood squarely on their feet: and the dying shook the mists of death from their eyes, and rose in their hundreds, dreadful to look upon, standing shoulder to shoulder with their living comrades, and all of them with one purpose in their hearts. When the attacking green wave of the enemy charged towards them, expecting little or no resistance, they were met by a solid scarlet wall of terrible men. And as the scarlet wall advanced towards them, slowly at first, but moving faster and faster, keeping time with the hastening "pim-pam-parradiddle" of the drum, they faltered uncertainly, with terror mounting in their hearts. Then they turned and fled, throwing down their weapons as they went. As they disappeared over the hill from which they had come, the "pim-pam-parradiddle" faltered, and Peter staggered and fell, shot through the heart by a stray bullet. But he had done his work. The battle was won.

They found him still crouched over his drum, clutching a single drumstick. The fairy one had disappeared.

The story of how Peter had saved the day, and the King himself on his golden throne, was told far and near. He was given a hero's burial, and the battered drum was treasured ever afterwards.

That was how Parradiddle Pete won Fame.

A sad story, you say? Well, that depends on how you look at it. But it is not quite the end. They do say that on moonlight nights, if you happen to be crossing Dundreary Moor, you may hear the ghostly "pim-pam-parradiddle" of Peter's drum, throbbing once more in that wild place: and if you listen very hard, just after each beat, you may hear a second, tiny tap, which might be an echo, or yet again might be "pim-pam-parradiddle", beaten on a drum no bigger than a teacup.

The Mermaid and the Monster

ONCE upon a time there was a little mermaid. As you know, mermen have very large families. This mermaid was the youngest of a family of as many mer-children as there are shrimps in all the rock pools from Southend to Weston-super-Mare. She was very small, but she was very pretty. Her hair was green as marram grass, her eyes were blue as sea holly, and her tail was gleaming silver, flecked here and there with little golden scales; but because she was the youngest of a family that was so very large, she had no name. No one could think of one that had not been used before. Because of this, when she was a mer-child, the other mer-children would leave her out of their games. This made her very sad. But how could she be chosen by any side if they had no name with which to summon her? And how can you play hide-and-seek if you have no name to guess when you are caught? Her brothers and sisters teased her and called her "Thingummy-jig" and "What-do-you-call-'em", and told her that such a very small mer-person could not expect to have a name.

When her youngest sister was about to be married the little Mermaid said:

"I wish you all the happiness in the great wide sea! How I look forward to the time when I shall marry someone just as kind and handsome!"

"Pooh!" said her sister. "Whatever would be the use of a wife without a name? You can be sure that no one will ever want to marry *you*!"

This made the little Mermaid more miserable than she had ever been before; and she swam away to her favourite distant rock, taking with her her little coral harp, which was the most precious thing she had, and with her pale fingers she twangled the strings of sea-horse hair, and sang a song which was so sad and so sweet that the hermit crabs were charmed from their shells, and the very sea anemones cried with her.

Not very far from the Mermaid's rock, deep down in a black sea hollow, lived a Monster. Now instead of legs, mer-people have tails like fishes, while from the waist up they are the shape of human beings. This Monster was the other way round. He had two legs instead of a tail, though these were covered with dingy scales, and from the waist up he was the shape of a fish; but the fishy part, instead of shining like a salmon or even a codfish, was covered with craggy knobs and nodules, and he had been sitting so long in his black sea hollow, that long strands of seaweed had taken root all over him. In the deep, dark hole in which he lived it was always night. The few fishes who swam there had eyes like searchlights, so that they could see where they were going in the surging darkness.

The little Mermaid's singing drifted down through the sparkling waves to the murky depths where the Monster lived, and he lifted his heavy head and listened, then with three kicks of his scaly legs, the seaweed streaming behind him, he rose from his dark hollow, up and up, and the water round him changed from inky black to dark green, and from dark to pale green. It grew lighter and more golden, until it was as clear as topaz. His scaly great head rose among the sparkling waves only a few feet from the little Mermaid's rock. He shaded his great red eyes from the sparkle of the waves with the shaggy fins that grew from his shoulders – for he was very short-sighted from sitting in the dark so long – and said:

"Tell me, little sea anemones, what is this singing that has made you weep, and has charmed the hermit crabs from their shells, and brought me from the black sea hollow I haven't left for half a century?"

The sea anemones stopped crying, and said rather crossly: "Hush, and listen!"

The Monster looked and saw the little Mermaid for the first time, and he heard her singing, while she twangled the strings of her little coral harp more sweetly than ever.

And he said to himself:

"How I should like to have a pretty little companion like that in my dark sea hollow! She could play on her coral harp and sing to me all day long! I think I shall ask her to be my wife."

He could not call her name of course, because she hadn't got one, so he clapped his fins together to attract her attention, but she took no notice. At first she thought it was nothing but the waves slapping against the rock. When at last she saw the Monster, she stopped singing in mid-note, she was so surprised.

"Who are you? And what do you want?" she asked.

"I am the Monster who lives in the deepest, darkest hollow of the sea where it is always night!" he growled; and he swam a little nearer to the craggy rock, and the Mermaid edged a little higher up. "I want you to marry me and come and live for ever in my deep, dark hollow, so that you can sing to me all day long

and twangle on your coral harp, for there is no one there to keep
me company save the fish with eyes like searchlights."

The little Mermaid edged still further up the craggy rock and
said in alarm:

"But I don't want to live for ever in a deep dark hollow at the
bottom of the sea! And if it is always night there, I shouldn't
know when it was day to sing to you. Besides, I should miss
sitting in the rock pools making wreaths of seaweed with my
sisters, and playing catch-as-catch-can through the breakers with
my brothers in the moonlight, even if they do tease. I should not
care at all for the company of nothing but a few fishes with eyes
like searchlights!"

"But as well as the fishes with eyes like searchlights, you'd always have *me*!" said the Monster, grinning horribly.

The little Mermaid only just had time to say to herself: "And that would be worst of all!" when the Monster made a pounce, as though to catch her. She just escaped him, and slithered to the top of the rock. But in doing so she dropped her coral harp, and it slid down the side of the rock with a harsh twanging of strings, slipped into the water and sank out of sight.

"Oh, my harp!" said the Mermaid. "It is the most precious thing I have, and now it has sunk to the bottom of the sea!"

"Then you'd better come with me and we will look for it together," said the Monster cunningly.

"Not I!" said the Mermaid, and she sprang into the sea, which had turned to a surly grey, with little caps of foam on every wave. For a moment the Monster's weak eyes were dazzled by the flash of her silver tail so that he could not see which way she had gone, so he cupped his shaggy fins round his great mouth and shouted:

"Mermaid, wherever you are! If you want your little coral harp, come back to-morrow at the same time, and perhaps I shall have found it for you!"

The Mermaid answered never a word, although she made up her mind to go back. She did so want her little coral harp.

That night there was a terrible storm. The thunder rolled and the lightning flashed. The hermit crabs crept back into their shells, and the sea anemones drew in their waving arms and clung to the rock for all they were worth; but next morning it had blown itself out. There was nothing left to show for it but the wreckage of a hundred ships floating on the heaving sea.

The little Mermaid swam back in good time to the craggy rock, and sat and thought how sad it was that no one wanted to marry her but the Monster, and she buried her face in her hands and cried.

Presently she was surprised to hear someone call: "Ahoy there!"

She looked up, and floating among the wreckage of a hundred

ships was a hen-coop, and sitting astride the hen-coop was a sailor, and he rode it as gallantly as though it was the most mettlesome sea-horse in her father's stable. He had hair the colour of a ginger biscuit, a great many freckles, and a merry eye.

"Well, blow me down, you must be a mermaid!" said the sailor in astonishment. "I've heard tell of such creatures, but I've never met one before. But why are you crying so sadly, and what is your name?"

At this the little Mermaid cried even harder than ever, and between her sobs she told the sailor that she had no name, and *that* was the whole trouble, and that no one wanted to marry her except the Monster, and she couldn't abide him, with his scaly legs and great red eyes: but that she did so want her little coral harp, which was the most precious thing she had.

"Dang me!" said the sailor. "Mermaids and Monsters and little coral harps, all in one afternoon, let alone a shipwreck! My name is Samuel Chipps, at your service, ma'am. Ship's carpenter to *The Jolly Arethusa*, lost last night with all hands in the terrible storm. You fish and me Chipps!" he went on, and slapped his thigh and laughed. The little Mermaid laughed too, though she didn't really understand the joke.

Samuel Chipps moored the hen-coop to the craggy rock and they talked together of this and that very comfortably, until the little Mermaid saw the boiling of the sea which showed where the Monster was going to appear.

"You'd better hide until he has gone," she said.

"And so I will!" said the sailor. "I'd like to have a dekko at this ugly great Monster of yours. But don't you go and marry him if you don't fancy the idea. Perhaps I may be able to help you. You never know your luck!"

Samuel Chipps hid behind the rock just in time to see the Monster's scaly head appear. The ugly creature shook the seaweed from his great red eyes and said:

"I searched and searched and at last I found your little coral harp!"

"Oh, thank you!" said the Mermaid, holding out her pale arms. "Please give it to me, and I will play you the prettiest tune I know!"

"Not so fast!" said the Monster. "I haven't brought it with me. I'm not so soft as that! I've hidden the harp where neither you nor anyone else will ever find it, in the darkest cranny of my deep black hollow, where it's so dark you would never be able to see it if you were only a fin's length away! For down there it is always as black as night. But if you marry me and come and live down below you shall have the harp for a wedding present, and then you can sing, and twangle on its strings to your heart's content!"

The little Mermaid thought quickly, and hoping desperately that the sailor could help her, she said:

"Give me a little time to make up my mind, Monster."

"I'll give you till this time to-morrow," he said. "Not a moment longer. And if you don't say Yes, I shall crush the harp to powder and use its strings for garters!"

When he had said this he sank beneath the waves in a swirl of bubbles, and Samuel Chipps came out from behind the rock.

"Well, he is an ugly customer and no mistake, and crafty, too!" he said. "I'd go and look for your pretty little harp myself, for I'm a mighty strong swimmer, if only I could breathe under the sea."

"If I were to tie a strand of my green hair about your left wrist, you could breathe under the sea as easily as though you were on dry land," said the Mermaid. "But suppose the Monster caught you?"

"If it's as dark as all that in those salt water parts, he won't be able to see me!" said Samuel.

"But neither will you be able to see the harp!" said the Mermaid sadly.

"Well, that's as may be," said the sailor. "I can but try."

So the Mermaid pulled out a strand of her green hair and tied it round his wrist and begged him to be careful, and he dived

into the heaving sea as neatly as any merman, and as he sank
through the swirling waves the colour of the water changed from
topaz to pale green, and from pale green to dark green until it
was as black as night. It turned out to be just as the Mermaid
had promised. He could breathe as comfortably as though he was
on dry land.

When he felt the cold clammy sand at the bottom of the
hollow beneath his bare feet he said to himself:

"It's true enough. I can't see a fin's length in front of my face,
I shall have to think of some other way of finding the harp, for
to *feel* my way round the Seven Seas would take a month of
Sundays."

He stood very still so that he could think the better, and
suddenly the deep sea silence was broken. He heard a noise that
was tuneless but musical, a faint, strange twangling sound, now
loud, now soft, according to whether the current pressed hard
against his ears or softly.

"The harp!" said Samuel. "The sea itself is playing on its
strings!"

First the sound seemed to come from one side, and then the
other, but as he cast about it grew louder and louder, so that he
knew he must be getting nearer. At last it became so loud that
it almost deafened him, and he put his hands over his ears and
said:

"If only I could have a light for as long as the blink of an eye –
so that I could see where the harp is!"

At that very moment one of the fishes with eyes like searchlights came swimming by, very slow and stately, and the two
beams from its great eyes swept over a high pinnacle of rock,
with the Monster fast asleep at its foot, and the coral harp wedged
in a cranny at the very top.

"Hi! Wait a minute!" called Samuel to the fish, but it took no
notice at all, and the two shafts of light slid away from the harp
as it sailed on its stately way into the darkness.

"Well, I can remember as near as no matter where I saw it,"

said Samuel. "But I must be careful not to wake the Monster!"

He swam carefully over the Monster and up towards the place where he had seen the harp for a fleeting second, and the sound of its wild music was all about him. He made a grab at the harp and caught it with his two hands and wrenched it from its cranny, but at the same time he felt a sharp pain in his left wrist.

"I must have scraped it on the rock when I made a grab for the harp," said the sailor. "What a good thing it isn't any worse. But what's this? I can't breathe any more!" And he felt his sore wrist. The Mermaid's green hair was gone! "Swim for your life, Sammy Chipps, with what breath you've got left!" he said. He kicked with his legs and shot upwards again, but as he did so his right foot became entangled with one of the strands of seaweed that grew from the Monster's head, and the creature woke with a roar; for it was just as painful as having your hair pulled.

The sailor untwisted the seaweed and swam on, and the Monster heard the music of the harp growing fainter as he swam away with it and gave chase, bellowing as he came :"Stop! Stop, thief!"

"Swim for it, Sam!" said the sailor faintly to himself for he had hardly any breath left. He swam through the water that was black as night and he had just enough sense left to button the harp inside his jacket – so that the sea should not be able to play on its strings any longer – although he felt as though a great boulder was pressing on his lungs. The Monster was close on his heels but he swam bravely on. When the water was turning green the Monster was even closer, but luckily for Samuel, when the green became pale as seaweed and he was swimming more slowly, for he felt as though the weight of a house was pressing on his lungs, the Monster became dazzled by the shining green, and with his short-sighted eyes mistook a walrus who was swimming past for the sailor, and went off in pursuit of him instead.

When Samuel reached the water that was pale as topaz he

was nearly done, for he felt as though the weight of the King's palace was pressing on his lungs. But the little Mermaid was looking anxiously for him, and when at last she saw his pale face appear above the surface with closed eyes, she saw how it was, and she plunged into the sea and dragged him up on to the craggy rock.

"I've – rescued – your – little – coral – harp – for – you," said Samuel, and then he fainted away.

When he came round again the little Mermaid was smiling down at him under a curtain of green hair.

"You are so very brave and clever," she said shyly, "I was wondering if perhaps you could think of a name for me?"

Samuel Chipps sat up and put his hand to his aching head.

"Shiver-my-timbers!" he said, and he was just going to add that until he could shake the sea water out of his eyes and ears and mouth he could not think at all, but the little Mermaid clapped her hands in delight.

"Shiver-my-timbers!" she repeated. "What an entirely new and delightful name! Now perhaps someone will marry me after all!"

The sailor laughed and said:

"I'm glad you like it." Then he stopped laughing. "As a matter of fact I should rather like to marry you myself. Will you be my wife? Then you can have another name as well!"

"Two names?" said the little Mermaid in wonder. The sailor nodded.

"If you married me you'd be Mrs Shiver-my-Timbers Chipps. But I should always call you Timbers. Will you be my wife, Timbers?"

The little Mermaid put her small pale hand in his large red one and said:

"I would marry you if *you* had no name at all!"

And so they were made man and wife. For six months of the year Samuel wore a strand of the Mermaid's green hair round his left wrist so that he could live under the sea, and for the other six months the Mermaid wore one of his ginger-coloured hairs round her right wrist so that she could live comfortably on land, and they were as happy as the sea is salt.

And the Monster? For all I know he is still chasing the walrus he mistakenly thought had stolen the little coral harp, for they never heard of him again.

Mrs Scruby and the Spanish Spider

ONCE upon a time, there was a poor old woman whose name was Mrs Scruby. She was a kind old woman, but there was one thing she could not abide, and that was spiders.

Because Mrs Scruby was so very poor, when something wanted mending in her tumbledown house, she did not call in the carpenter, or the plumber, or the man who mends the roof. She managed by herself in the best way she could. The front-door bell was tied with a piece of string, and every night when she went to bed, she put three tin basins on her bedroom floor to catch the water that trickled through the ceiling if it rained. The drips went "Plink! Plank! Plonk!" as they fell into the basins, sometimes so loudly that Mrs Scruby could not get a wink of sleep. When this happened she would go downstairs and brew herself a cup of tea.

One day the two cords broke that made her kitchen window go up and down.

"Now how in the world can I mend those?" she said to herself. "I shall just have to prop up the window with a piece of firewood. I do so like a nice airy kitchen."

Mrs Scruby managed to prop the window up, but when it was time to go to bed, she found it had become wedged so firmly that she couldn't let it down again.

"I don't think it matters," she said to herself, as she lit her candle and stumped up the creaking stairs. (The lights had all fused long ago.) "There isn't a thief alive who is thin enough to get through such a very small gap. Besides, who would bother to burgle a little old house with the door bell tied with string and so many holes in the roof?"

She put the three tin basins on the bedroom floor, in case it should rain in the night, and she climbed into bed, pulled the bedclothes about her ears and went fast asleep.

Mrs Scruby was quite right. There was no burglar living thin enough to squeeze through the gap at the bottom of the kitchen window; but something else could!

In the middle of the night it began to rain quite hard, and the drips went "Plink! Plank! Plonk!" so loudly in the three tin basins that she could not get a wink of sleep, so down she went to brew herself a cup of tea. She had no five-penny pieces for the gas meter, so she stirred the fire and boiled the kettle, and she was just going to pour the water into her little brown teapot, when what should she see sitting inside on the window ledge but a big black Spider!

"Lawks!" screeched Mrs Scruby. She was so startled that she dropped the teapot lid, and it fell on the floor and was broken into a thousand smithereens.

Now it happened that the Spider had come all the way from Spain, by mistake, in a crate of oranges. Mrs Scruby could see he was a Spanish spider by the golden ear-rings in his ears. She could also see that he was very wet and shivering with cold.

"After the orange grove in which I was born and bred," said the Spider sadly, "where the sun shines all day, and the cicadas sing, your yard seemed so very cold and wet! I saw the red eye of your fire winking in a friendly way, so I ventured to come just inside . . ."

"Then, you can just venture outside again!" said Mrs Scruby angrily, shooing him with the skirt of her flannel night-gown. "Spanish spiders indeed! I don't care if you come from Timbuktu! You made me drop the lid of my little brown teapot so that it is broken into a thousand smithereens. Away with you! Shoo!"

The Spanish Spider crept sadly out into the wild, wet night, and Mrs Scruby poured herself a cup of tea: but she did not enjoy it very much. Without a lid to the pot it was not nearly hot enough. So back she went, rather crossly, to her warm, cosy bed.

The next night it was colder, but she stuffed the gap at the bottom of the window with newspaper.

"I'll give him Spanish Spider!" said Mrs Scruby, and she climbed into bed, pulled the bedclothes about her ears and went fast asleep.

Presently it began to rain harder than before. It beat upon the window pane like a shower of half penny pieces, and the drips went "Plink! Plank! Plonk!" in the three tin basins, so that Mrs Scruby could not get a wink of sleep. So down she went to brew herself a cup of tea. She found the top of an old tin to use, instead of the teapot lid, and she was just going to pour the milk into the cup with a pattern of pink roses, when what should she see sitting on the edge of the draining board but the Spanish Spider, with his golden earrings winking in the firelight!

"Lawks!" screeched Mrs Scruby. She was so startled that she dropped the little china jug. "You bold bad Spanish Spider! You made me drop the lid of my little brown teapot last night, and now my little china jug, so that they are both broken into a thousand smithereens. I thought I had stuffed up the window with newspaper so that you couldn't get in!"

"It was so very wild and wet outside," said the Spider. "I saw the red eye of your fire winking in a friendly way, and I found a little cranny that I could just manage to creep through . . ."

"Then you can just creep yourself outside again!" said Mrs Scruby, and she flapped angrily with the floor cloth with which she was mopping up the spilt milk. So the Spider crept sadly out into the wild, wet night.

Mrs Scruby drank the cup of tea, but she did not enjoy it very much, for she had no more milk: so she stumped, rather crossly, up the creaking stairs and climbed back into her warm, cosy bed.

The next night it was colder still, but she stuffed the gap at the bottom of the window with the floor cloth.

"I'll give him Spanish Spider!" said Mrs Scruby, and she climbed into bed, pulled the bedclothes about her ears and went fast asleep.

Presently it began to rain even harder than before. It beat against the window pane like a shower of penny pieces, and the drips went "Plink! Plank! Plonk!" in the three tin basins, so that she couldn't get a wink of sleep: so down she went to brew herself a cup of tea. Mrs Scruby poured the milk straight out of the milk bottle because her little china jug was broken, and she was just going to put three lumps of sugar into the cup with a pattern of pink roses, when what should she see half-way across the kitchen floor but the Spanish Spider, with his golden earrings winking in the firelight!

"Lawks!" screeched Mrs Scruby. She was so startled that she dropped her best blue sugar basin. "If it isn't that Spanish Spider again! You've made me drop the lid of my little brown teapot, my little china jug and my best blue basin, so that they are all broken into a thousand smithereens, and I thought I had filled up the gap at the bottom of the window with the floor cloth so that you couldn't get in!"

"It was so *very* wild and wet outside," said the Spider. "I saw the red eye of your fire winking in a friendly way, and I found a little chink that I could just squeeze through . . ."

"Then you can just squeeze yourself outside again!" said Mrs Scruby angrily, flapping the dust-pan and brush at him, with which she was sweeping up the sugar lumps. So the Spider went sadly out into the wild, wet night, and Mrs Scruby drank the cup of tea. But she did not enjoy it very much, for she had no more sugar: so she climbed crossly up to her warm cosy bed again.

The fourth night it was colder than ever, but Mrs Scruby wedged her rolling pin at the bottom of the window, and it seemed to fit the gap exactly. "There's no burglar or Spanish Spider in the world who can get round that!" she said triumphantly. "I'll give him Spanish Spider!" And she climbed into bed, pulled the bedclothes about her ears and went fast asleep.

That night it was colder and wetter still, and the rain beat against the window pane like a shower of ten-penny pieces, and the "Plink! Plank! Plonk!" of the drips in the three tin basins wouldn't let Mrs Scruby get a wink of sleep, so down she went to brew herself a cup of tea.

She poured it out of the little brown teapot with the tin lid, and she trickled in the milk from the milk bottle because her china jug was broken, and she took three lumps of sugar from the leaky cracked cup she had to use because she no longer had a sugar basin, and she was just blowing on the tea in the teacup to make it cool enough to drink when what should she see but the Spanish Spider, as bold as brass, sitting beside her on the hearth rug, with his golden earrings winking in the firelight!

She was so startled that she dropped the china cup with pink roses, and it fell on the floor and was broken to a thousand smithereens, and the tea trickled hissing into the fire.

"Lawks!" screeched Mrs Scruby even more angrily than before. "You've made me drop the lid of my little brown teapot, my little china milk jug, and my best blue basin, and even my china cup with the pattern of pink roses, so that they are *all* broken to a thousand smithereens. I stopped up the gap at the bottom of the window with my rolling pin so that you shouldn't get in. I thought it just exactly fitted!"

"Not quite!" said the Spider. "Since I left the Spanish orange grove in which I was born and bred, where the sun shines all day, and the cicadas sing, I have grown so thin that if there is a crack at all I can get through with the greatest ease."

"Not through my window you don't! Not again!" said Mrs Scruby in a towering rage, and she picked up the Spider by one of his thin legs, and she took away the rolling pin, and she prodded him out through the gap on to the window ledge. Then she shook the window so angrily that the wedge of firewood fell out and the window came down with a bang, and she stumped up the creaking stairs dusting her hands on her flannel nightgown and muttering:

"Spanish Spiders indeed! This time I think I've done for him. But what a long time it is since I really enjoyed a cup of tea!" She climbed into her warm, cosy bed, and pulled the bedclothes about her ears – but she did not go to sleep. She lay and listened to the drips falling into the tin basins, and instead of saying: "Plink! Plank! Plonk!" as before, they seemed to be saying: "Poor! Cold! Spider!" over and over again. Mrs Scruby pulled the bedclothes even tighter about her ears, but she could still hear the drips saying "Poor! Cold! Spider!" She listened to the rain driving against the windows like a shower of fifty-penny pieces.

"What a terrible night it is to be sure!" said Mrs Scruby.

Presently she could bear it no longer. She got out of bed and went down the creaking stairs, and pushed up the window: and there was the Spider curled up into a wet, unhappy ball outside.

"You can come into the warm if you like," said Mrs Scruby. "I've been a cross bad-tempered old woman!" And she carried the Spanish Spider very carefully over to the hearth on the palm of her hand. "My, my, you certainly have grown thin! Why, you weigh no more than a tea leaf! What can I give you to make you grow fat again?"

"Dear Donna Scruby," said the Spider, from his warm place on the hearth, and he blew her a polite Spanish kiss with his two front feet. "What is this 'tea' that you make in the middle of each night, and why do you drink it?"

"I drink it in the night to make me go to sleep," replied Mrs Scruby. "And – well, I drink it in the morning to wake me up."

"Caramba!" said the Spider. "If it sends to sleep and also wakes up in the morning, it must be a very powerful magic drink. I should like to try a cup of tea!"

Mrs Scruby said: "You have made me drop the lid of my little brown teapot, my little china milk jug, my best blue basin and my cup with the pattern of pink roses, and I haven't got another, so we shall just have to drink out of the saucer."

She stirred the fire till the flames danced again, and she boiled the kettle and warmed the pot and made the tea, and in the empty cake tin she found just one crumb of cake which was exactly the right size for a spider.

"It's a funny thing," said Mrs Scruby presently, as she sipped the steaming tea, "but although the little brown teapot has a tin lid in the top, and I've poured the milk from the milk bottle, and taken the sugar from an old leaky cup without a handle, and here we are drinking turn and turn about from the saucer, yet it's the best cup of tea I've tasted for a month of Sundays! I suppose it's because I've got company to share it with!"

The Spanish Spider nodded. He couldn't answer because his mouth was so full of cake.

Sammelkin

ONCE upon a time, in the days before people were in too much of a hurry to listen when animals spoke to them, in the green heart of England there lived two brothers called Thomas and Timothy. They were both very poor, and they were both cobblers, and they had both set their hearts on marrying Mistress Hepzibah, the Squire's daughter, although neither of them had so much as spoken to her. But there the likeness ended: for Timothy was hard-working and cheerful, while Thomas did no more than he could help, and was always grumbling. One cold rainy day, when Thomas had been complaining even more than usual, Timothy said:

"My dear Thomas, I know as well as you how poor we are. But we've a lot to be thankful for. We've got a warm fire and a roof over our heads . . ."

"And we shan't have that for long!" interrupted Thomas. "All the leather we have left is just enough for us each to make one single pair of shoes! And when that is used up, how shall we pay the rent?"

Before Timothy could answer, there was a knock on the door. When he opened it, outside in the cold and rain stood a little old woman. She wore a faded blue cloak and a tattered scarlet petticoat, but the frills that framed her wrinkled old face were crisp and white, and the eyes that peered up at Timothy were bright as a robin's.

"Come in out of the cold!" said Timothy. "And warm yourself by the fire!"

"Thank you kindly," said the old woman. "I lost myself by Willerby Tarn, and besides, I had to come all the way on foot."

"And how did an old body like you expect to come?" said Thomas rudely. "By coach and six horses?"

"Stranger things than that have happened," said the old woman coolly. "My mount went lame."

"I hope you've left no half-starved animal to run loose over our cabbage patch!" said Thomas.

"My Esmeralda would have little use for cabbages, Thomas Trant!" replied the old woman, and Thomas wondered how she came to know his name. "I'm on my way to Stonecrop. They say the best withies for mending brooms grow there."

"Ten miles further on!" said Timothy. "And all to mend an old broom?"

"There's brooms *and* brooms, young man!" said the old woman.

"Well, you can't go as far as that with your shoes worn to tatters!" said Timothy. "You slip 'em off, mother, and toast your toes by the fire, and I'll have them patched and mended and good for twenty miles in no time at all!"

"Don't be a fool!" said Thomas. "If you use your share of the leather for patching and mending you won't have enough left to make even one pair of shoes. That's our only piece of leather."

"And I expect that's the old woman's only pair of shoes," said Timothy. "And you needn't pay me, mother," he said to the old woman.

"I'll pay! Make no mistake about that, young man!" she said, her bright black eyes darting from one to the other of the two brothers.

When Timothy had finished the shoes she slipped them on again.

"H'm, as good as new, they are. Thank you kindly, Timothy Trant. And now you've only enough leather left to make a single shoe. But you never know, even one shoe may come in useful.

As for payment, it won't be in money, but it'll be useful none the less for that!"

As she spoke the old woman opened the door and whistled shrilly down her fingers, and called high and clear: "Sammelkin! Sammelkin!" And down the path between the borders of stocks and sweet williams stalked a great black cat; a battered-looking creature, with one fierce yellow eye and a torn ear.

"I've a new master for you, Sammelkin, my poppet, just for a season," she said. "I mean the young chap with a kind heart over there. You can't conjure kindness where it don't belong, no matter how strong your abracadabra. A little warmth and comfort will do you no harm for a season. Take care of him, Timothy, for he's all I've got. He'll serve you just as well as you serve him. I'll be back for him again come Hunter's Moon."

"A mangey old cat!" grumbled Thomas. "And only lent at that. Another mouth to feed. Is this what we deserve?"

The old woman interrupted sharply:

"You shall have what you deserve, both of you! Make no mistake about that!"

She brushed all that was left of Timothy's share of leather with a long gnarled finger, and said something they neither of them heard. Then she nodded, put her shawl over her head, and the two brothers watched her walk briskly down the garden path.

"Good gracious!" said Thomas. "It's not a horse or a donkey she's untying from the gate post, it's a broom!"

"So it is!" said Timothy. "Just look at it, nuzzling her shoulder and following her down the road like a pet lamb!"

"I'm beginning to wish I'd been ... well, a little more gracious," said Thomas uneasily. Sammelkin looked up from the hearth rug and said quite distinctly:

"Gracious? Downright rude you was, Thomas Trant!"

"Mercy on us!" said Thomas. "A broomstick that walks, and a cat that talks! Then the old woman *must* have been a witch! If only I'd known!"

"You'd have been a deal more civil, I don't doubt," said Sammelkin drily. "But she works fast, does my mistress. I wouldn't be surprised if that isn't someone's deserts coming up the path this minute!"

As Sammelkin spoke there was a brisk rap on the door, and when they opened it, who should be standing on the doorstep but Miss Hepzibah herself, the Squire's daughter. Very tall and slim she looked in her green riding habit, tapping impatiently with her riding crop.

"Is no one going to open the door and ask me in?" she said haughtily. "They told me I should find a cobbler here. I've a nail as big as a marlin spike in my riding boot."

"Oh, please to come in!" said Thomas and Timothy, falling

over themselves in their eagerness. When they had hammered down the nail, and polished the riding boots so that Sammelkin could see his whiskers in them, Mistress Hepzibah put them on and announced herself satisfied.

"Tell me," she said. "Do you make shoes as well as mend them? You do? Then I've an idea I should like to try you. You shall each of you make me a pair of shoes for my birthday ball which is on Saturday six weeks. They must fit as snug as a mouse's skin, and look as neat, for that matter, and I will wear one pair until midnight, when I've no doubt I shall have danced them through, and with the second pair I shall dance till dawn."

As she spoke Sammelkin fenced and parried with the end of her riding crop, as graceful as an otter, so that Mistress Hepzibah threw back her head and laughed. "This is a clever cat!" she said. "Bring the shoes in good time, and there will be a mug of beer for you both with the servants, and a saucer of milk for Sir Pusskin here!"

And she tossed the brothers a silver sixpence and went away laughing.

No sooner had she gone than Thomas dug his brother in the ribs and said: "Do you hear that, my boy? Shoemaker to Mistress Hepzibah! And who knows what that may not lead to? It'll be Squire's shoes next, and all the gentry round! Why, my fortune's as good as made! What a pity you haven't enough leather left to make a pair of shoes!"

"Then I shall just have to make *one*!" said Timothy.

"You're never coming to the Hall with *one* shoe, and disgrace us before the company?"

"Of course we're coming," said Sammelkin. "Both of us. I were asked along of you, weren't I? For what else do you think I did all them silly capers with the riding crop at my time of life?"

"This is too much!" said Thomas, nearly crying with rage. "My fortune as good as made, and then to have it snatched away by – by a lunatic brother and a common witch's cat. I won't stand it, I tell you! I shall go away. I shall hire myself out to the new shoemaker in the town. And if you dare to appear at the Hall in six weeks, with your single shoe and your one-eyed cat, I shan't own you, so there!"

Thomas tied his few belongings up in a bundle and went stumping off without another word, slamming the door behind him. He hired himself out to the smart young shoemaker in the town, and in a very short time was in a fair way to becoming as much of a rogue as his master. But the first thing he did was to make the dancing shoes for Mistress Hepzibah. You would go a long way before you found a prettier pair of scarlet slippers: but the leather was of the cheapest, and the stitching was neat only where it showed.

In the meantime Timothy and Sammelkin lived on in the tumbledown cottage, making a meagre living by mending the villagers' boots and shoes with what scraps of leather Timothy could find. But every evening he spent making the single shoe for Mistress Hepzibah.

On the night of the ball Timothy wrapped the single shoe in a napkin, stuck a pink in his hat and set off for the Hall with Sammelkin trotting at his heels.

When they got there the fun was in full swing. Timothy joined the crowd of servants at the ballroom door and looked in. The room was ablaze with wax candles whose light fell on all the dashing young men and lovely girls for miles around, and all of them footing it for all they were worth. But the most beautiful was Mistress Hepzibah herself, with her black curls dancing as nimbly as her scarlet slippers. Timothy was suddenly aware that someone was trying to squeeze in among the watching servants. At first he thought it was a child.

"Here, you can stand in front of me, my dear," said Timothy. And then he saw that it was not a child, but a young girl. "Perhaps you can tell me who some of the grand people are?"

"Oh yes, if you please, sir," said the girl. "That's young Squire Wurzle dancing with Mistress Hepzibah. Sweet on her they say he is. Such beautiful presents as she has had! Eighteen to-day she is. And that's Parson talking to old Squire, of course. Very quick-tempered, Squire is, with a voice like a bull, for all he's such a snippet of a man. But that's because of the gout, they say. Keeps one foot done up in a great bandage propped up on a stool all day."

"And who are you?" asked Timothy.

"I'm Janey, if you please," said the girl. "The under-kitchen maid, and Cook said I could come and see the grand sights just for five minutes, for I'm eighteen too to-day!"

"Then here is a birthday present for you," said Timothy. And he took the pink from his buttonhole and gave it to her. And very pretty she looked when she blushed and tucked it in her hair.

"Now tell me," went on Timothy. "Who is the fine gentleman standing over there by himself? I seem to have seen him some-where before."

At this Sammelkin sniggered rudely. "It's enough to make a cat laugh!" he said. "Look again, master!"

Timothy gave a gasp. "Why, it's Thomas!" he said. "How grand he looks! Silk stockings and a velvet waistcoat, almost like a gentleman! But what has happened? Why have the fiddlers stopped?"

There was a crowd round Mistress Hepzibah, who was standing in her stockinged feet in the middle of the floor.

"What's this? What's this?" said the Squire, limping up as fast as he was able with his gouty foot. "Why has the music stopped, hey?"

"Because I can't lead a dance with no shoes to my feet!" said his daughter angrily. "My scarlet slippers have split at every seam, and I've only worn them for an hour! As for the second pair I ordered from the other rogue of a shoemaker, he seems to have forgotten all about it!"

"That he hasn't!" said Timothy, and he elbowed his way through the crowd. "Here I am, and I've done my very best shoemaking for you!" As he spoke he unwrapped the single

slipper and held it up for all to see. But there was a titter from the company, and Mistress Hepzibah's black eyes flashed.

"Did I order clogs for milking cows?" she asked furiously.

"Oh no," said Timothy. "But it would not hurt if you did milk the cows in it! It is strong as well as neat. I only wish I had had enough leather to make a pair."

"Do you mean to say you've only made a single shoe? You impudent rogue!" began Hepzibah. But the old Squire broke in:

"Now wait a minute! This is what I call a real shoe! Not the kind of rubbish you wenches wear for jigging in. Why, I could wear it myself . . . even on my gouty foot!"

And the Squire slipped the shoe on his gouty foot. Although it looked far too small it fitted as snugly as a mouse's skin.

"Well, what are you waiting for?" he said. "Hepzibah, tell

the musicians to strike up again, and dance in your stockings! And you shall hop about with the best of them, young man!" he said to Timothy.

If Timothy danced with the kitchen maid, and not Mistress Hepzibah, he had to admit it was the evening of his life! They danced till the sun rose and made the candles look like ghosts of stars in their silver sconces, and the flower in Janey's hair drooped against her flushed cheek. Timothy went home with five golden guineas in his pocket, and an order for a pair of riding boots from the Squire, for the old man had danced the evening through in his new shoe with all the prettiest girls, without a twinge of gout. And Sammelkin? He made friends with a young she-tabby cat who showed him where the cream was kept, and I don't know which of them enjoyed themselves most, Timothy, the Squire, or the witch's cat.

"But take my advice, young master," said Sammelkin when they got home. "Do you keep every scrap of the leather you made the shoe from, however scrappity it may be."

The weeks went by, and Timothy made many boots and shoes for the Squire. This meant frequent visits to the Hall to fit and measure. Although he seldom saw Mistress Hepzibah, he generally contrived to have a word or two with Janey, the under-kitchen maid. At the same time Thomas did a brisk trade among the servants, making them shoes that were as smart as they were uncomfortable. But although he made much more money than his brother, Thomas was bitterly jealous of Timothy.

One day Timothy arrived with a new pair of riding boots for the Squire, who was dressing in his closet. The little old man sat with his wig on its stand, and his great gold watch beside him on the table. He looked very different from the gouty, bad-tempered Squire Timothy had first seen at the ball. He was as active as a robin and lean and brown with healthful exercise. He slipped on the boots and nodded approval and said:

"You're a good shoemaker, Timothy. Your boots are so comfortable that now I can spend all day in the saddle. I'm grate-

ful to 'ee, very, but for a week or two you'll have to put up with
gratitude instead of money. Squires can be poor as well as
cobblers. Look at the carpet, threadbare – and the plaster dropping
from the ceiling like ripe fruit. Do you remember when I put on
your shoe at the ball I said I'd give all I had to be rid of my gout?
It's almost as if someone heard me. For I've been as spry as a
two-year-old ever since, but at the same time I've been losing
money. It's nearly all gone now, and the odd thing is I don't
mind – cheerful as a cricket. It's Hepzibah I'm sorry for, for she's
been brought up a fine lady. But what's all this to you? Get along
with you, young man. You shall have your money just as soon
as I've got it. Hey, day."

It was a very thoughtful Timothy who walked slowly down
the wide stairs. So thoughtful was he that it was not till he was
half-way home that he noticed that Sammelkin was not trotting
behind him as usual. He turned and looked back, and there was the
black cat, two fields away, running like the wind.

"Here's me straining every paw to catch you up in time!"
said Sammelkin. "To save you from stocks and prison bars!
While you was with Squire, who should be measuring Cook for
a new pair of shoes but that brother of yourn. Yellow nankeen
breeches and all. 'A *leetle* higher in the heel,' he says. 'As worn by
the Duchess of Doodle.' And Cook taking it all in enough to
make a cat laugh!"

"But what is all this about stocks and prison bars?" asked
Timothy.

"Squire'ses gold watch has been stolen, that's what. And you
the only one who could have done it, they say. But it weren't
you," said Sammelkin.

"Of course it wasn't me!" said Timothy indignantly. "Whoever could it have been?"

"I've got a clue!" said Sammelkin mysteriously. "A little bit
of yellow nankeen!"

"Why, what's the good of that?" said Timothy.

"Now, listen to me and don't interrupt," said Sammelkin.

"After a little matter of cream with that young tabby cat, when you'd gone to see Squire, I cleans my whiskers and goes up them little dark back stairs, to see if you'd gone without me. And while I was going up someone coming down 'ustles me. I 'ates to be 'ustled, so I lets fly with my clawses and thinks no more about it till I finds you'm gone and they starts hollerin' about Squire's gold watch. Then what should I find in my left front claw but a piece of yellow nankeen! And who wears yellow nankeen breeches, may I ask?"

"Why, my brother Thomas!" said Timothy.

"They think you stole the watch because you were the only person as had been in Squire's room. But p'raps you wasn't. Him as come down them back stairs must 'ave been there too. It don't lead nowhere else. But I must prove it. When you're took up to Squire, go quiet, and leave everything to me!"

So Timothy was taken before the Squire who put him in the stocks as a thief, with his feet held fast, so that when all the village came to make fun of him he could not stir. When at last they grew tired of this and went home, who should come sauntering up but Thomas?

"My poor brother!" he said. "What a sad end to all your hard work! Who would have thought when the old woman said you would have what you deserve, that she meant the stocks? Of course *I* only make shoes for the servants, but perhaps when you are in prison things will change and I shall work for Squire as well!"

"You don't seem to be doing so badly as it is," said Sammelkin. "That's a fine pair of yellow nankeen breeches you'm wearing. Pity you've tore a hole in the seat."

"So vexing!" said Thomas. "An unknown ruffian attacked me the other day in the dark."

"The unknown ruffian were me," said Sammelkin coolly. "And I've got the little bit of nankeen that just fits the hole to prove it. Squire will be quite interested when I goes and tells him it was you what stole the watch!"

"You'd never do that to me?" said Thomas in alarm. "I should die if I was sent to prison! I only did it because I was jealous of you, Timothy! I'll make amends! I'll put the watch back, and perhaps Squire will think he just mislaid it somehow. If only you won't get me into trouble!"

"Very well," said Timothy. "If you do that, so that nobody any more thinks I am a thief, why, we'll say no more about it."

"But I don't trust you from here to the village pond," said Sammelkin to Thomas. "You gets out of this village by sundown, or I ups to the Squire and tells him all I know!"

So Thomas put the watch back and off he went. The Squire, who felt he'd been unjust to Timothy, was kinder than before.

The weeks slipped by, till once more the cottage garden was filled with stocks and nasturtiums and Michaelmas daisies. Timothy was now quite prosperous. But as he grew richer, the Squire seemed to grow even poorer.

"Do you think Mistress Hepzibah would look at me now, Sammelkin?" said Timothy one day. "I've a good mind to go and ask her if she'll marry me this very minute!"

So he put on his best clothes, scarlet waistcoat and all, and went up the weedy, moss-grown drive to the Hall. Standing at the shabby front door was a handsome canary-coloured coach.

"Who does this grand coach belong to?" Timothy asked the coachman.

"Why, to Sir Thomas Trant, the rich city merchant!" said the man.

"Sir Thomas Trant? And has he been knighted long?" asked Timothy in surprise. "Why do you laugh, coachman?"

"Because he ain't never been knighted, so far as I know," the man replied. "But 'e says he's bound to be soon, so there's no harm in calling himself 'sir' a bit early!"

Timothy and Sammelkin walked thoughtfully up the steps and into the empty hall, and hearing voices in the shabby, unswept parlour, they walked in, and there was the Squire looking completely nonplussed. For who should be kneeling before his daughter but Thomas, so dressed up in lace and velvet, and his hair so crimped and curled, that only Sammelkin and Timothy recognised him. Timothy walked straight up to the Squire and said:

"I have come to ask for your daughter's hand in marriage."

But Thomas broke in:

"Do not listen to the fellow, sir! Now *I* can offer the position due to a baronet's lady: your own coach and as many fine clothes as you can want, mistress. May I hope . . .?"

"Lady Hepzibah Trant!" said the Squire's daughter. "Yes, that sounds very well! I am quite willing to be your wife, Sir Thomas!"

And with Hepzibah on his arm, mincing like a poodle, Thomas led her away; and in three weeks they were married.

That evening, instead of going on with his work, Timothy sat in the porch watching the great golden moon sail over the trees at the end of the barley field. Presently something else sailed over the trees: a black shape that grew bigger and bigger. Sammelkin arched his back and made little croodling noises in his throat.

"Why, it's the little old woman on her broomstick!" said Timothy.

She landed beside him as gently as a feather.

"Well, young man," she said as she dismounted. "It's Hunter's Moon, so here I am. Both you and Sammelkin here look fat and sleek. I said you and your good-for-nothing brother should have what you deserve. Are you satisfied?"

"I've money enough," said Timothy sadly. "But it's Thomas who has married Mistress Hepzibah."

"Bless the boy!" said the old woman. "I suppose you think you should have married the Squire's daughter? Fiddlesticks! Now fetch the leather that was left from the single shoe you made, no matter how small the pieces, and make yourself a pair of shoes with them. The moon's bright enough to see by!"

So Timothy fetched the leather, and oddly enough, although

they seemed such little pieces, there was just enough to make himself a pair of shoes. He slipped them on, and they fitted as snug as a mouse's skin, but before he could say a word they ran away with him as fast as lightning. Down the road they went, and up the drive to the Hall, past the front door, pausing for a moment under a lighted window. Inside, Timothy could hear Thomas and Hepzibah quarrelling together, hammer and tongs! But the shoes would not let him stay. They whisked him away again, round to the back of the house to the only window with a light in it. And there he saw Janey, the only servant the Squire had left, washing up a great pile of dishes by the light of a single candle, although it was two o'clock in the morning.

"Good gracious, what a fool I've been!" said Timothy. "What do I want with Mistress Hepzibah?" And he popped his head through the window and said:

"Janey love, will you marry me?"

And Janey looked up from the pile of dishes and said shyly: "Dear Timothy, I don't mind if I do!"

Which was her way of saying there was nothing in the world she would like better!

Benno and the Secret Code

BENNO lost the only written copy of 3b's Secret Code the term that the feud between 3a and 3b was at its height. He still says it was not his fault.

It happened in the school library one Friday evening after lessons, when he was choosing a book to read for the week-end. Wally Green passed him a single sheet of paper with the double wink that meant "Feud business!" He couldn't *say* anything for two reasons: one was because there were four boys from 3a standing near: the other was because there was a large notice on the Library wall which said "SILENCE". Mr Bates sat at a desk in the corner, waiting to take down the names of the books that were borrowed. He seemed to know exactly who was just going to whisper to someone else, even before they spoke. He would suddenly say sharply: "No talking, please, Peter!" or "Paul", or whoever it happened to be, without even looking up from the books he was correcting.

As soon as Wally had given the Secret Code to Benno he hurried away. Benno was sure that the enemy 3a boys had seen the transaction by the way they looked at him. They were nudging one another and grinning. They could hardly have failed to guess that something was up, because when Wally winked he screwed up his whole face, as though he was sucking a very sour lemon.

"What on earth shall I do with it to keep it safe?" Benno asked himself, as he fingered the precious piece of paper. "It mustn't fall into enemy hands, and if I keep it in my pocket those 3a stinkers will probably lie in wait round the corner, and give me a good old frisking when I get out of here." (They were still looking at him and grinning.)

Then Benno had what he thought was a brilliant idea. He pulled out the nearest book in front of him, slipped the Secret Code between the pages without anyone noticing, put the book back where it came from and sauntered out of the Library.

As it happened no one followed him after all.

"But they might have done," he explained to Wally and the others in the cloakroom. "But it's as safe as houses where I hid it, and I've only got to go back and collect it when the Library opens again on Monday afternoon."

"You're sure you know which book you put it in?" asked Wally.

For the first time Benno began to feel a little uneasy, but he said:

"Well, not what it was called exactly, but it was red, and on the fourth shelf up, just opposite that big ink splodge on the floor. I can find it as easy as pie."

"You'd better!" said Wally. "If anyone in 3a gets the book out and finds it first, I wouldn't be in your shoes, Benno Brown!"

By now the Library was closed, so Benno couldn't go back and show just how easy it would be to find it. There was nothing to do but wait until Monday. He spent a rather anxious week-end.

You may be sure, Benno was the first into the Library on Monday afternoon. He hurried over to the ink splodge on the floor, took down the book he felt it must have been, and riffled the pages. The paper was not there. He took down another, and another, slapping each one carelessly back into its place as it failed to produce the Secret Code, until Mr Bates said sharply:

"You are not playing hoop-la, Benno! Kindly treat those books with respect! I spent the whole week-end rearranging the shelves, and I don't want them muddled up again."

"Rearranging the books, sir?" said Benno, with a sinking heart. Mr Bates nodded. "It seemed to me," he went on, "that many of

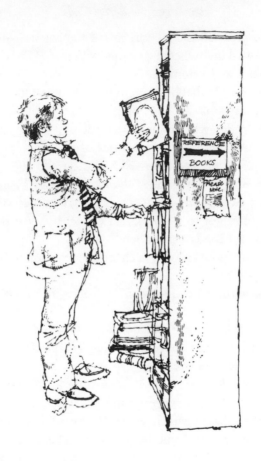

you read only the lighter, worthless stuff, and if I arranged them in order of subjects instead of authors, you might, in your search for them, be persuaded to read something more serious. What's the matter, boy?"

Mr Bates was strict but not unkind, and he saw that Benno was unhappy. "Was it some special book you wanted?"

"Oh, yes!" said Benno eagerly. "I wanted – "

And there he stopped, because he realised that he didn't really know what he wanted.

"Well, if you don't know the name of the book, what was it about?" asked Mr Bates.

"I don't know, sir," said Benno miserably. "It was – Oh, it doesn't matter." And he slunk unhappily from the Library.

Wally and the others were waiting for him in the cloakroom.

"Well, have you got it?" asked Peter Pratt. Benno shook his head. He explained what had happened.

"But it's there somewhere. It must be!" he said.

"Then you'd jolly well better find it!" said Wally.

There was a confused murmur from the knot of boys, from which Benno made out such ominous words as "letting down the form", and "traitor to the cause". Suddenly Peter Pratt said:

"Well, I vote we send him to Coventry until he finds it!" There was a murmur of approval from the others.

"But how shall I do it?" asked Benno miserably. "I can't look through every book in the Library, there must be hundreds!"

But, of course, no one replied, even if they knew the answer, because, if you are sent to Coventry, it means that no one is allowed to speak to you for any reason at all. Unless it has happened to you, and I hope it has not, you can have no idea how wretched it can be.

As no one would speak to him in the classroom, or the cloakroom, or the playground, Benno took to hanging round the doors of the Library even when it was closed. He was the first in at four o'clock, and the last out when it closed at four-thirty. But in all the red books he hunted through, and he started with the top row just inside the door, he found no trace of the Secret Code. Mr Bates began to look at him suspiciously.

"I didn't know you were so interested in books, Benno," he said on the third afternoon.

"Oh, I am, sir! I am!" said Benno eagerly.

"It all seems rather sudden," said Mr Bates. "Well, perhaps in that case, you might like to be Library Monitor until Edward Jones recovers from whooping cough?"

"Oh, thank you, sir!" said Benno. "I should love to!"

This would double his chance to search the shelves, he thought, sometimes with the room to himself.

"Then that's settled," said Mr Bates. "Your job will be to dust the shelves, tidy the Library when everyone has gone at four-thirty, and make a note of the books that are borrowed, should I be called away for any reason."

Benno carried out his duties as Monitor, but, as you can imagine, at the same time, whenever he got the opportunity, he searched and searched. But *still* he could not find the Secret Code; and *still* no one in 3b would speak to him.

On Monday afternoon at four-fifteen, a week after Benno had been sent to Coventry, Mr Bates looked at his watch and said:

"I have an appointment to see the Head, so I shall have to leave you in charge. Hardly anyone comes on Mondays, but you had better take my place at the desk in case they do. Enter the name of each book that is taken out in the register, and the name of the boy who chooses it. And your best writing, mind!"

As soon as he was alone Benno sat down, rather gingerly, in the master's desk. At first he pretended to be Mr Bates, and said:

"No talking there, Wally Green!" several times, in his best Mr Bates voice, keeping his eyes fixed on the desk as Mr Bates did.

It was then that he saw the magnifying glass among some rubber bands and a few paper clips, in the lid of an old cardboard box. He picked it up and fixed it in his eye. It was a remarkably powerful magnifying glass, which made the tiny ridges of the desk top look like a ploughed field, and the pencils great baulks of timber. He turned it on to a round tin box which was labelled Drawing Pins, and at the same time he distinctly heard a minute voice say:

"Help! Help! Let me out!"

Benno was so startled that he dropped the box and the magnifying glass at the same time.

"I must have imagined it!" he said to himself. But the minute he screwed the glass in his eye again, so that the small tin box looked almost as large as a hat box, he heard the voice again.

"Let me out!" it cried.

Very gingerly Benno took the lid off the box and looked inside. There, clinging to an upturned drawing pin, was a little wisp of a worm, no thicker than a thread of gossamer. It was such a pale grey that it was almost transparent. In fact he felt it was only just there at all. Its eyes were large and bright, with markings like spectacles round them, and its forehead was high. Its mouth kept up a constant munching movement, rather like a cow chewing the cud.

The little creature looked up at Benno and said:

"Human Sir! Food, food, I beg you! I am starving!"

"What sort of food do you want?" said Benno in bewilderment.

"What sort of food do you think bookworms usually eat?" it replied tartly.

"Bookworms?" said Benno in amazement. "But I thought bookworms were only . . ."

"Then you thought wrong!" broke in the little creature sharply. "Bookworms eat books, of course! Though anything in print will do at a pinch. Not too indigestible after so long starvation, please. But hurry. A whole week, and not a page or paragraph has passed my lips!"

Benno put his hand in his pocket and pulled out a comic paper, and put it on the desk. In doing so he dropped the magnifying glass. Without it he could no longer see or hear the bookworm.

"I suppose in some way it magnifies my hearing as well as my sight!" he said to himself. Hurriedly he put it back in his eye. With fingers that looked through the glass like large, not very clean pink sausages, he picked up the drawing pin with the bookworm clinging to it, and put it carefully on the comic paper. At once, there was a faint scrunching sound, such as a fly-sized rabbit might make chumping a miniscule lettuce, and in no time at all, the bookworm disappeared down a hole of its own munching, a hole so small that even with the magnifying glass it could only just be seen, only to come up again through another, with a tiny "pop!".

"Yarooh!" it said as it reappeared. "I sure was glad of that, pard!"

"Good gracious!" said Benno to himself. "It's begun talking like my comic!"

"Yoweeee!" went on the bookworm. "A bit of grub in the old bread-basket does do a power of good . . . But," here it hiccuped slightly, "I was really brought up in the classics. Hic! Pardon! . . . Do you think you could . . .?"

Benno turned in his seat – it was the kind that swivels round – and took a book at random from the shelf behind him. It happened to be a copy of *Treasure Island*. At once there was the same faint, tiny munching noise, as the bookworm disappeared down a hole in the cover, exclaiming as it reappeared:

"And a bottle of rum!"

"I'm sorry," said Benno. "I haven't any rum."

"I don't really want it," said the bookworm. "It's just part of the song. You missed me singing the 'Yo-ho-ho!' part."

"I see," said Benno. "Do you always talk in the language of the book you have just been eating?"

"Of course!" said the bookworm. "And no wise bookworm mixes his reading if it can help it. Though don't think me ungrateful. It can bring on terrible fits of stammering. But, Human Sir, you have saved me from a dreadful fate. What can I do to reward you?"

Benno was seized with a wild hope. He told the bookworm about the missing Secret Code.

"You used it as a book-mark?" the bookworm asked. "Book-markers are the bane of bookworms. That is how I fell into that dungeon full of spikes." (Benno realised that he meant the box of drawing pins.) "There was I, quietly munching my way through *Alice in Wonderland*," it went on, "when, without any warning, I ran my head against a sheet of silver paper someone had used as a book-mark, and carelessly left behind. Of course, no bookworm can eat that. Stunned myself completely, and I must have fallen into that dungeon place, and not come round till the lid was on. Horrible!"

"It isn't a book-marker that I've lost," explained Benno. "It's something much more important, written on a sheet of paper torn from a rough notebook. I hid it there to keep it safe . . . and now I don't know which book I put it in! I don't see how even *you* could find it among all these." He waved his arm at the book-lined shelves.

"Not unaided," said the bookworm. "But you don't imagine that I am the only inhabitant of the shelves? Good gracious, no! I am the Oldest Bookworm in the Library, and therefore of some authority. Be patient, young Human Sir, just watch and listen!"

So saying it reared itself up on its coiled tail, threw back its head, and made a noise like the kind of Indian war-cry contrived by patting your mouth with the palm of your hand as you call. The bookworm, of course, had no hands, but the constant munching of its jaws had the same effect. It was the highest, shrillest sound Benno had ever heard.

At once, from every side of the Library came the noise of innumerable little "pops", like the sound of hundreds and hundreds of dress fasteners being pulled apart, as from the spine of every book in the Library, three or four bookworm heads appeared.

Benno watched in astonishment. They wriggled out and down on to the shelves, where they joined together in little drifts and flurries, which, if he had not known better, he would have thought no more than shifting dust. Down to the floor they clambered, and up to the top of Mr Bates's desk, where they re-formed into companies, as the Oldest Bookworm explained, according to the kind of books they lived in.

"Brothers!" said the Oldest Bookworm, when they had all assembled. "Listen to me! I have to-day been rescued from death by starvation by this noble Human Sir!" He waved his head at

Benno. There was a stir among the crowd round him. "This Human Sir is himself in trouble, from which we alone can save him. Shall it be said that we bookworms are ungrateful?" A cry of "No! No!" went up, by bookworm standards in a mighty shout, though to Benno it was nothing but a whisper. "Silence, for the noble Human Sir!" said the Bookworm, and the pushing and eddying of the crowd ceased. Benno explained how he had hidden the paper with the Secret Code written on it inside a book.

"Tell us, Human, tell us true,

What it is you'd have us do?" asked a poetry bookworm.

"Why, find the book I hid it in, if you are able!" said Benno.

"Doubt not, Human Sir!" said a historical-novel-burrowing bookworm. "Zounds! Thy task is as good as done!"

But a soldierly-looking war-bookworm at once took charge.

"Gad, sir!" he said. "This must be conducted as a military operation. Leave the organising to me!"

The assembled host swirled round the war-bookworm, who climbed up on to the lid of the drawing pin box, and said:

"Back to your shelves, chaps! Start from left to right in open munching formation! The first to find a page he can't pronounce, to report at once!" He turned to Benno. "Respected Human Sir! The troops have their marching orders. They are brave fellas, and I've no doubt will do their duty. But they have many hours of munching ahead. If you return to-morrow at sixteen-thirty hours, Operation Secret Code should be completed. Now then, chaps!" he went on, turning to the bookworms once more, "Action Stations! Forward march!"

And to the faintest of strains of the march, "Stars and Strips Forever," hummed by a company of music-bookworms, they filed back to their shelves; and then the humming faded into an all-pervasive steady munching sound which seemed to come from every corner of the room.

At that moment Mr Bates came back. Benno took the magnifying glass from his eye, and at once all was silence.

"Sorry I've been so long, my boy," he said.

"That's all right, sir," said Benno.

"Anybody been?" asked Mr Bates.

"Hundreds and hun – I mean, no, sir!"

You may be sure that Benno hurried to the Library the minute the four o'clock bell went the following day, even though he knew he must not expect anything to happen until four-thirty. There were a number of boys choosing books. The room looked disappointingly as usual, and the shelves bare of everything except books.

"But of course they are!" said Benno to himself, "until I've got the magnifying glass to look through again. I hope to goodness it's still there!"

To his relief, it was. Unfortunately, so was Mr Bates. However, under cover of showing him a book whose back needed mending, Benno was able to slip the magnifying glass into his pocket, and hurry to a corner where he was unlikely to be noticed and fix it in his eye. Even then he could not see so much as the flip of a tail of a bookworm. There were some half-dozen boys choosing books, and though of course they did not talk, the shuffle and bump they made as they walked about and chose what they wanted to read made it impossible to hear if there was a sound of munching going on or not. Had he imagined the whole thing, Benno wondered? Desperately he looked at his watch, which seemed through the magnifying glass as large as the Town Hall clock. It was four-fifteen, and now there were only six boys in the Library. Never did watch-hands move so slowly! At four-twenty-five there was only one boy. Benno thought he would never go. At exactly four-thirty he went. Mr Bates was absorbed in his correcting. There was not a sound to be heard, even with the magnifying glass in his eye. Benno's heart sank to his boots. He *must* have imagined the whole thing! And then the rustling began, and a faint, faint sound of singing. Along the length of the shelf by which he stood, he saw what at first he took to be a flurry of dust, but as it came nearer he saw it was a mighty company of bookworms gliding towards him, shoulder to shoulder, led by a massed choir of song bookworms singing "John Brown's Body," because it was the most triumphant song they could find. The Oldest Bookworm was at their head.

"Greetings, Human Sir!" he said to Benno, signalling to the song-bookworms to stop singing. "I think we have found what you have been searching for. It is in the fifteenth book from the right on the third shelf down on the left of the Library door. It was discovered by one of our youngest members. Come along, now," he said to a very small bookworm who was wriggling shyly at his side. "Tell the noble Human Sir what you read at the top of the piece of paper."

The tiny creature looked up shyly at Benno and said, "Aw, shucks!" for he was a Wild West bookworm by nature. And then he said just two words:

"TIRKEES EDOK"

And, with a flood of relief, Benno knew that the Secret Code had at last been found. If you study these two words carefully you will see why. He was so excited that he clean forgot where he was.

"Whoopee!" he shouted. "I don't know how to thank you! I think you're the most wonderful . . ."

But Mr Bates's voice broke in.

"What on earth are you doing, boy? Talking to yourself in a corner! And for heaven's sake, you don't have to look for dust on the shelves with a magnifying glass! Give it to me, at once!"

Very slowly Benno took the glass from his eye, and watched it disappear into Mr Bates's pocket, where it probably lies to this day. But, of course, the sound of the massed choir of bookworms singing "John Brown's Body" (for they had started again) stopped abruptly, as though turned off with a switch, and the shelves were empty once more of everything except books.

"Please, Mr Bates, sir!" said Benno eagerly. "I want to take a book out. May I have that red book, fifteenth from the right on the third shelf down on the left of the Library door?"

"Bless the boy!" said Mr Bates irritably. "I don't want to know its geographical position! What is it called?"

"*Mactavish's Commentary on the Bible*," said Benno, squinting hurriedly at the shelf.

"Are you sure that's the book you want?" asked Mr Bates incredulously.

"Oh, yes, quite, sir!" said Benno.

"Well," said Mr Bates. "Wonders will never cease!"

But he handed over the book to Benno, and there, between pages fifty-one and fifty-two, was the Secret Code.

The Stone People and the Alderman

IN a small country town there is a fat and self-important looking Alderman, who lives in the middle of the Market Square, with his back to the small but beautiful cathedral, and his front to the Gas Works. All day long he stands in his Alderman's robes, with the fingers of one hand pushed firmly between the second and third button of his marble waistcoat. In fact, he is, as you will have guessed, a statue. As you would expect, he is there all day. But after moonrise, now that is a different matter!

When this story begins his statue had only just been unveiled. If anyone had been watching carefully while the unveiling ceremony was going on, they might have noticed that as the Mayor and the Councillors were making speeches, about what fine fellows they all were, and the Alderman in particular, the bump under the dust sheet that covered him, (which might have been made by the marble nose of the Alderman,) was moving gradually higher and higher; almost as if he was feeling more and more pleased with himself as he listened. And when with a crashing of the brass band and a cheering of the townspeople, the covering was finally tweeked away by the Mayor, there stood the Alderman on his pedestal in his marble robes, with his chest thrown out, and his nose pointing in a nor' westerly direction by the weathercock on the top of the Town Hall, but with an even prouder upward tilt than the sculptor had ever intended.

There the statue stood when the Mayor, and the Councillors, and the brass band, and the townspeople, and the sculptor went home to tea. The sun set, and the sky turned from primrose to indigo behind the towers of the cathedral, and the street lamps in the distance started out of the darkness, in pale imitation of the stars. Not that the Alderman noticed any of these things. Dear me, No! He was far too busy thinking that although the Mayor had said some pleasantly complimentary things about him in his speech, there were one or two places where he might have said a good deal more. Now when the moon had sailed so high that it looked as though it was spiked on the tallest spire of the cathedral, the Alderman started quite unpleasantly when he heard a voice coming from below the curve of his waistcoat.

"Hi!" said the voice. "You up there. Who are you?"

The Alderman lowered his affronted gaze from the roof of the Gas Works, so that his chin almost disappeared inside his collar, and there looking up at him was a small boy, dressed in nothing but a small pair of marble wings, who looked very much like one of the marble cherubs from the cemetery.

"Don't be impertinent, child!" said the Alderman, who was not used to being addressed as "Hi!" "If you want to know who I am you have only to read the inscription carved on my pedestal. Well? Why don't you read it?" he went on irritably.

The boy looked puzzled. "Read?" he said. "What is that?"

"You mean to say that you don't know what reading is, at your age? Disgraceful!"

With great dignity and some puffing, the Alderman climbed down from his pedestal, all ready to give the winged child a lecture. After all, was it not by his speeches that he had become an Alderman? But before he had even finished clearing his throat ready to begin, the boy turned and shouted:

"Ho, there, brothers! Here's a strange new statue come to join us! Come and see!"

And from the dim Cathedral, the Town Hall, the Market Square, from the Museum and the Art Gallery and the public park, came walking and running, dancing and skipping, shadowy white figures who collected round him in a whispering crowd.

"Thank you, good people," said the Alderman, hurriedly

deciding on a gracious speech, instead of a scolding one. "It is kind of you to come and welcome me. I can only think that my humble reputation has gone before me!" And he puffed out his chest in a way that was anything but humble. "But even here I shall not remain idle," he continued. "I see that there is much to be done. I shall speak to the school authorities at once about the shockingly ignorant state of some of the younger members of our community." (That was his way of saying children.) As he spoke he frowned at the winged boy, who had been joined by a number of smaller children dressed in nothing but wreaths of flowers, who were laughing, and munching the fruit they carried in curly-shaped stone horns. *They* looked very much like the statues from the refreshment rooms in the Public Gardens.

"I shall certainly recommend serviceable shoes, and some sort of school uniform," the Alderman went on, looking with disapproval at the stone children who were too busy giggling and throwing grapes at one another to take any notice.

There was a murmur from the crowd as they were joined by the stone water-nymphs from the fountain in the Market Square, a strange pack of carved animals from the Cathedral, and the marble figure of Britannia from the Town Hall.

"I also feel it my duty," went on the Alderman, who was warming nicely to his speech, "to protest against this custom of going about in . . . fancy dress. Disgraceful! You, sir!" he added, pointing a plump marble finger at one of the armour-clad Crusaders from the nave of the Cathedral. "You, sir, I repeat, are old enough to know better!"

There was an indignant murmur from the crowd, which surged forward to the bottom step of the statue. In front was Britannia's lion, followed by a couple of gargoyles from the Cathedral roof.

"Really, madam!" spluttered the Alderman as he climbed hurriedly back to his pedestal again, "it isn't safe to keep pets like that! They should all be under lock and key in the Zoo!" And he nervously drew his marble boots out of reach of the oncoming animals.

Luckily for the Alderman, at that moment the Crusader whistled down his fingers and the creatures paused, and like a pack of well-trained hounds they came to heel.

The Crusader laughed a deep rumbling laugh, and said:
"Fat and foolish old man! You have much to learn. The first thing is that we are as the Sculptor made us. You yourself, sir, whether you like it or not, are now one of the Stone People. We have our own laws here. Before you can be received into the Brotherhood, at least one of three things must be proved."

The Alderman straightened his tie and confidently smoothed his marble hair.

"Is he beautiful?" asked the Crusader, turning to the Stone People.

"No!" shouted the crowd.

"Are you useful?" he continued. "Can you be used as a fountain, or a sundial, or a seat, or even a water spout?"

The Alderman drew himself up haughtily.

"Certainly not!" he said. "I am an Alderman!"

"Beware!" said the Crusader. "Unless you can show that there is some reason for your existence, the Stone People will have none of you. This is your third and last chance. Have you ever done anything really useful in the past?"

There was a hush in the moonlit square. The whispering died down, and the stone animals edged forward expectantly. The Alderman smiled a self-satisfied smile and said:

"Most certainly! I have sat on the Town Council for seven years!"

"And what did you do there?" asked the Crusader.

"I – I – er, made speeches," said the Alderman irritably.

"Words! Words! Is that all?" said the Crusader. "Think well, old man! Have you perhaps done something else that is *really* useful? Have you ever made anything with your hands?"

"Good gracious, no!" said the Alderman, who thought that to use his hands was beneath his dignity.

The Crusader nodded.

"I know your kind," he said. Then turning to the crowd he shouted: "Are you satisfied, Stone People? Is he worthy to join the Brotherhood?"

He was greeted with a roar. "No!" they shouted, and they surged towards him.

And the Alderman, doubt in his marble heart for the first time, turned and leaped from his pedestal, and took to his marble heels. After him pelted the crowd, headed by the stone beasts.

"Gently!" said the Crusader. "He is old and foolish. Only teach him a lesson."

The Alderman ran, with the stone creatures at his heels. Through the square he went, his marble robes billowing behind him, round the Town Hall and the Gas Works, through the moonlit Public Gardens, with its empty fountains and deserted pedestals, up the High Street and down Memorial Row, with the stone creatures in full cry after him. And as he ran, he said to himself: "Have I perhaps *not* really been useful in the past? It may be that I am not *quite* so handsome as I liked to think. I only wish I could think of some way of being useful in the future!"

His pursuers did not catch him. Perhaps they never meant to; but fear lent speed to his marble boots. When the sky began to lighten and his strength to give out, the Alderman headed desperately for the Market Square again. Just as he took a flying leap back on to his pedestal, with a couple of gargoyles from the cathedral roof hanging on to the skirts of his robe, the golden weathercock on top of the tallest spire crowed shrilly. At the same time the Crusader whistled down his fingers, and in a flash the Square was empty of all save the statue of the Alderman, and the first, sleepy shaft of sunlight.

Each night the same thing took place. The Stone People collected round his pedestal, and with less and less assurance, the Alderman gave the same answers to the same questions. And then the same chase began. And every night, as he ran he thought to himself:

"The past is over and done and can't be altered. If only I could think of some way to be useful, now and in the future!"

On the thirtieth night, when the moon was full once more, he said breathlessly to himself as he ran:

"I-wonder-if-that-would-do? I-can-but-try."

And on the thirty-first night, as the questioning started again, and the stone animals were ready to spring once more, he held up his hand and said:

"Good people, I pray you listen to me for a moment! I freely admit that I am not beautiful, but as you have said, we are as the Sculptor made us. Nor have I done much of value in the past, I see that now. But perhaps it is not too late, and I can still be of use for something. Please . . ." And he looked imploringly at Britannia and the Crusader. "Sir and madam, will you kindly step up and take a look here?"

As he spoke he pointed to his marble Alderman's three-cornered hat which lay up-turned at his feet, and there inside, cocking a round and shining black eye, was a sparrow sitting on a nest of eggs. She twittered sleepily as the Alderman stooped and stroked her soft brown head.

"Gently!" said the Crusader. "Do not disturb her."

And without a word the Stone People tiptoed away.

In time the eggs hatched out, as handsome a brood of baby sparrows as you could wish to see. If you are lucky enough to be there at the right time, you may see the Alderman sitting on the steps of his pedestal, with the winged boy on one side, chatting in a friendly way with the Crusader or Britannia on the other: but in the daytime, when you see him standing as you would expect, with his back to the Cathedral and his front facing the Gas Works, there will undoubtedly be a couple of sparrows, or a pigeon or two, sitting perkily on his shoulder or roosting by his marble boots.

The Duchess of Houndsditch

ONCE upon a time, in the days before there were such things as diesel engines and every train went by steam, there was an engine called the Duchess of Houndsditch, and she was as dear to her engine driver, William Bloggs, as a bicycle is to you. Every day he rubbed her brass trimmings till they shone like fairy lights, and he polished her plum-coloured sides till they glowed like red cough mixture. But his real pride was her whistle. As clear as a bell it was, and so moving that not a signal on the line could resist her.

It happened one day that the station master sent for William Bloggs, and said that in a few days' time a Very Important Person would be travelling on his line, and that the Duchess had been chosen to carry him, because of her musical toot.

William was delighted. Here at last was fame!

Now the Duchess had one failing. She was rather flighty, and she chose this of all times to start a grievance.

"Why," she said to herself, "must I, every day of my life, be fed on nothing but lumps of hard, knobbly coal, and green greasy train-oil?"

As they bowled along through the outskirts of the town towards the open country, she got quite worked up about it.

"It's a shame, that's what it is," she said to herself. "Here am I bursting my boilers to give satisfaction, and for what? Coal and train-oil, day after day. If only I could have some . . ." and here she looked round rather vaguely, for she didn't really know what she wanted. By this time they were well out into the country.

On either side of the track were wide pastures, lush with grass and yellow buttercups, on which cows were peacefully grazing.

"If only," said the Duchess, "if only I could browse on lush green grass and yellow buttercups."

In a short time they stopped at their first station. It was a neat, well-kept station with the name marked in Virginia Stock in the flower-bed as well as written on the seats and placards.

William, like the porter of the station, was a keen gardener, and to-day, as on many days, he left the train for a few minutes' chat about his vegetable marrows. This gave the Duchess her chance; she had noticed beyond the signal-box a meadow, full of brown, contented cows, browsing peacefully on lush green grass and yellow buttercups. The station was empty except for the station cat stalking flies, and without thinking twice she undid her couplings, picked up her pistons, and crept quietly away. A few cows looked up in mild surprise when she lumbered rather heavily into the field. They had no objection, it seemed, to her joining them in a little lush grass and yellow buttercups.

"But chew your cud well, dear," volunteered the nearest cow. "Buttercups is bilious if you aren't used to them."

The Duchess thanked the cow for her politeness, and did her best to appear as though she were enjoying her meal. She put away enough to make a small haystack, and then she decided that perhaps the kindly cow was right about buttercups. She was feeling rather queer. Back on her line, securely coupled once more, she felt better. As luck would have it, she got back just as William Bloggs reappeared with a parcel of seedlings done up in damp newspaper.

Off they went once more, the Duchess a bit slow on her regulator, but all went well till they came to the next signal. William was anxious to make up for lost time, and this particular signal was the oldest and most obstinate on the line. It would hold up an express as soon as look at her. But William only smiled as he pulled the whistle cord. "Now ask him nicely, old lady," he said confidently.

There was a pause, but no whistle; only, from somewhere, so close that it might have come from the cab itself, came an unmistakable "Moo!"

William Bloggs started. There was not a cow in sight. But why was it that the Duchess had not tooted? He pulled the whistle cord again, harder this time, and again there came a prolonged and dismal "Moo-o-o!"

The signal stood bolt upright in shocked amazement. Could it be that the rich colour of the Duchess's rounded sides flushed to a deeper crimson? With an anxious heart, William Bloggs waited till in its own time the signal at last deigned to go down and let them through.

That night, for the very first time, they were late. William drove the Duchess straight into her shed. Perhaps a night's rest would put her right.

Next morning she refused to touch either coal or train-oil. William clicked his tongue unhappily. The Duchess off her feed! Such a thing had never happened before. But at the usual time they set off again, and William hoped for the best.

The truth of the matter was that the Duchess was sulking. Not that she had much enjoyed the buttercups, but there were other things in the world to eat, she said to herself, and there was William Bloggs giving her the same old coal and train-oil again. As the train climbed to higher ground, the buttercup fields became fewer, and their place was taken by meadows full of sorrel and round white daisies. There were no cows here, only soft sheep with frisking lambs in black woolly gaiters.

"That's what I want!" said the Duchess defiantly. "Sorrel and round white daisies!"

She watched her chance. When the train stopped at the next station, William Bloggs went to pass the time of day with the signalman, whose wife brewed such excellent herb beer. The Duchess slipped away quietly and unobtrusively to the nearest field. The sheep were not so polite as the cows had been, and some of the lambs were downright cheeky. Defiantly the Duchess

put away even more daisies than she had buttercups the day
before, and so quickly that she was hiccuping slightly when she
got back to the line. William Bloggs, wiping his mouth with the
back of his hand, hoisted himself up into the cab a few minutes
later.

Presently they came to the same obstinate signal. William put
a nervous hand on the whistle cord, and pulled. There was a
pause. Then, horror piled on horror, she did not whistle like an
engine, or even moo like a cow. The only sound which met his
ears was a long-drawn "Ba-a-a!"

Again William Bloggs was late. This time he was seriously

worried. What was he to do? In two days' time they were to carry the Very Important Person.

Next day William got out at the third station on the line and went to see the station master. His name was Perkins, and he was an old friend. William Bloggs had stood godfather to all the little Perkinses. The kitchen was bright and cheerful, with geraniums in the window, and a canary singing its head off in a cage. William found its whistle strangely comforting, because it reminded him of the Duchess's own lost voice. Mr Perkins chatted of this and that, but William was too worried to keep his mind on the conversation.

Presently Mrs Perkins said: "Whoever's gone and let the hens out? They're all over the platform. And, William, wherever is your engine?"

William Bloggs rushed out. There was no sign of his beloved engine, only half a dozen hens scratching hopefully on the dusty platform. He looked wildly round; there in the little hen-run behind the station master's house was the Duchess of Houndsditch. She was watching a young cockerel very closely, and apparently trying to scratch up the ground with her back driving-wheels. Every now and then she ducked clumsily as a hen might to peck at a grain of corn.

"Duchess!" roared William Bloggs in a voice of thunder. The Duchess started guiltily. "Get back to your line, Miss!" Now it was the first time that he had ever spoken harshly to her, and she was so surprised that she obeyed at once. As the train went on again, William Bloggs thought hard. Without waiting to reach the obstinate signal, he pulled the whistle cord, and it was just as he feared, the Duchess gave neither hoot, moo nor baa, but a loud "Cock-a-doodle-doo!" William did some more thinking. She had been eating corn with a cock and now she crowed. Yesterday he had found bits of daisies in the cab as though someone had been playing she-loves-me-she-loves-me-not with the petals, and she had baa-ed like a sheep, and the day before that there had been a couple of battered buttercups sticking out of her safety valve, and she had moo-ed like a cow. Clearly if she was to make a respectable engine noise again, she must be persuaded to take her proper train food. But might not that merely restore her voice to an ordinary everyday engine level? What could he give her to restore her whistle to all its old wild beauty? Somewhere at the back of his mind he remembered hearing a sound in Mr Perkins's kitchen which had been familiar and reassuring. Then he remembered, and his worried face relaxed into a smile.

That night he gave the Duchess no coal or oil. Instead, he talked to her very sternly about turning up her blast-nozzle at the good coal provided when many an engine would be glad of it. At first she twirled her bogie-wheels defiantly, and pretended that she didn't care. But presently she began to feel ashamed of herself, for she was a good-hearted creature really, and what's more, she was feeling very, very empty. It was a meek Duchess of Houndsditch who finally went to her shed that night.

The following morning William polished her brass work till she twinkled like the Milky Way; then he rubbed her sides till they glowed like stained glass with a sunset behind it. Next he gave her the finest and richest train-oil available, and a great heap of shining coal, every lump of which he had hand-picked himself, and mixed with the coal was a hundredweight of canary seed. William watched anxiously. It all disappeared: every drop of oil, every fragment of coal and grain of canary seed. What would be the result? But there was no time to waste in worrying, for they were due even now to meet the Very Important Person. Off they started, amid the click and whirr of cameras, the cheering of the crowds and the playing of the town band; past meadows full of cows and yellow buttercups: past the station where all the little Perkinses were lined up cheering and waving flags: past the hen-run, on and on, until they came to the difficult signal. Would it dare to hold up a train with a Very Important Person on board? But it did. With his heart in his mouth, William Bloggs put up a trembling hand, then: "Let him have it, old lady!" he said, as he pulled the whistle cord, and the Duchess whistled. The sound rose true and steady in the morning air, neither moo, baa, nor crow, but an exquisite whistle which both compelled and enchanted at the same time.

The signal quivered and fell without protest. The Very Important Person so far forgot himself as to pop his head out of the window. William Bloggs sighed with relief. "Good old Duchess!" he said, as she sped happily on to the terminus. There would be more crowds at the end of the journey: more speeches and more cameras, and who knows, even a microphone into which his darling Duchess might whistle to the listening millions!

Moggie Mewling

ONCE upon a time there was a bold sea Captain, who ruled his
four-masted schooner as a king his kingdom, both wisely and
well; except when some small thing went wrong – and then he
lost his temper.

One day he was pacing the quarter-deck, smoking an after-
breakfast pipe, and thinking what fine fellows were his crew,
and what good speed his ship was making with a following wind,
when quite suddenly his pipe refused to draw. He frowned and
puffed, and puffed and frowned, till he grew quite red in the
face; but still it would not draw, and he stopped feeling what
fine fellows were his crew. Then he pulled his large watch from
his pocket and roared:

"Mister Mate! The morning watch is over, and I expect my
ship to work like clockwork! Here we are in complete disorder!
Decks muddied like a ploughed field, and ropes in heaps like

your granny's knitting! See to it, sir! At the double!" And then he growled: "If that was not enough to plague a man, my pipe won't draw!"

"Ay, ay, sir!" said the Mate; but inside he was angry, for the only mark on the snow-white, newly-swabbed deck was where the Captain himself had knocked his pipe out, and the only rope not neatly in its place was the coil the Captain himself had kicked in his irritation as he passed.

"And all because his pipe won't draw!" muttered the Mate.

Now because the Captain had made him so angry, the Mate looked round for someone to work off his ill-temper on, so he called all hands and roared at them:

"Swab the decks again, and coil down the ropes, you lubberly, slovenly band of rascals!" And he roared so loudly that he made his voice quite hoarse. "You there!" he croaked to a passing Seaman, "If you can't jump to it faster than that, up to the crow's-nest with you, and see how fast you can go! If you're not down again by the time I've counted twenty . . . One . . . two . . . three . . . !"

Now the crow's-nest is the look-out on the top of the tallest mast, and when the Seaman had raced hand over hand up the rigging to reach it, he took out his handkerchief to mop his face, for the sun was hot. It was the only one he had, and it had been given him by his sweetheart Sue, but alas, the wind tugged it from his hand, and it whirled away to starboard, only to fall into the sea among the fishes. "And much use they'll have for it!" said the Seaman angrily to himself. But he had no time to stare after it, for the Mate had already got to "Ten!" So down he climbed hand under hand, and was only just in time. Because he was so angry at the loss of his handkerchief he looked round for someone to work off his ill-temper on. On his way to find a piece of cotton waste instead to mop his face, he came across the Ship's Cook, who was trying to thread a needle with which to darn his bedsocks, because his feet grew so cold in his hammock at night, and the Seaman shouted rudely to the Cook:

"Suetty pud again to-day, I'll wager, and heavy enough to sink a ship of the line as usual!"

The Cook was so surprised that his needle came unthreaded again. He prided himself on the airy lightness of his suet puddings, so that he was hurt and angry with the Seaman, and he looked round for someone to work off his ill-temper on, and he roared at the Cabin Boy:

"To the galley with you, instead of playing marbles, and peel me twice as many potatoes as yesterday! If you leave so much as a single eye among the lot of 'em, I'll . . . I'll make you walk the plank!"

Now the Cabin Boy did not say, "Ay, ay, sir!" but "Bother!" (under his breath) because of all jobs potato peeling was the one he disliked most. But as he pulled out a great sack of potatoes he stumbled over the Ship's Cat, and because he was angry with the Cook and wanted to find someone to work off his ill-temper on, I am afraid he kicked the Ship's Cat, who had come to see what her friend the Cabin Boy was up to.

Now the Ship's Cat was not much to look at, with one torn ear, and whiskers at sixes and sevens: but she had knocked about the world since she was a kitten, and had learned to take things as they come.

"What's a kick or two between friends?" she said to herself. She felt sorry for the Cabin Boy as she watched his scowling face as he bent over his work. "I'll change *that*, before the next ship's bell, or my name isn't Moggie Mewling!"

So she started patting one of the chips of peel that were showering down right and left, and she patted it and flipped it, and tossed it in the air, and pounced and parried, as though it was a mouse. And the Cabin Boy looked up and saw her, and first he grinned, and then he laughed out loud.

"You are a proper caution, Moggie Mewling!" he said.

And he stopped peeling with his little sharp knife for a moment, and rubbed her behind the ear. "I'm sorry I kicked you, puss. I

really am!" And he whistled quite gaily as he went on peeling, faster than ever.

When he went to tell the Cook that he had finished, the Cabin Boy found the old man standing by a port-hole still trying to rethread his needle, and he said:

"Here's twice as many potatoes as before, and not an eye between 'em. But give me the needle and I'll thread it for you."

He threaded the Cook's needle in the twinkling of an eye, and the Cook said:

"Thank you, my boy, you aren't such a bad lad after all. I think we'll just give 'em baked tatties for a day or two, to give you a rest from peeling."

As the Cook set off to fetch some currants to make a specially airy suet pudding, he happened to pass the Seaman who was trying to mop his face with a bit of cotton waste, and he said:

"That's no way to set about it! If you haven't got a handkerchief, you can have a bit of pudding cloth and welcome!"

The Seaman took the pudding cloth and swabbed his face and thanked the Cook. Just then he heard the Mate trying to give orders to the Bo'sun, but he was so hoarse that he could hardly speak. The Seaman felt in his pocket, and went up to the Mate and said:

"Begging your pardon, sir, but if you suck one of these here cough-drops, given me by my sweetheart Sue, it'll do your throat a power of good!"

With his mouth full of cough-drop the Mate nodded and said, "Thank you! Thank you, my good man!"

As he spoke he picked up a long sea-gull's feather that had fluttered to the deck, and he tiptoed to the quarter-deck where the Captain still stood, purple in the face with trying to make his pipe draw, and said:

"You might try cleaning your pipe with this, sir."

The Captain took the feather and poked it down the stem of his pipe, and at once the pipe began to draw again.

"Thank 'ee, thank 'ee, Mister Mate! Very kind!" said the Captain, beaming all over his face. "What a beautiful day it is! What excellent speed we are making, and what fine fellows are our crew! I think we'll pipe all hands and splice the mainbrace!" Which as every sailor knows means an extra tot of rum all round.

And Moggie Mewling? She did not fancy a tot of rum, so the Cabin Boy gave her a saucer of flying fish stewed in oil, with shrimp sauce, which made her purr like the Roaring Forties.

And that's all; as the whale said when it had swallowed the sprat.

THE END

About the Author

BARBARA SLEIGH lives in London with her husband, the former head of BBC radio's Children's Hour, where she also worked as a script writer. Since the closing of children's programs on radio, Miss Sleigh has concentrated on writing books, several of which have been televised. Among the many successful books she has written are JESSAMY; CARBONEL, THE KING OF THE CATS; and THE KINGDOM OF CARBONEL.

Miss Sleigh has one son and two daughters and says that her special interests are "cats and grandchildren—my own and other people's."